YEAR ONE: THE LAST WAR

THE FIRST WORLD OF DREI COLLECTION

ASHLEY POLLARD

Year One: The Last War

This is a work of fiction. All the characters and events portrayed in this short story are fictional, and any resemblance to real people, artificial super intelligences or incidents is purely coincidental.

A Triode Press publication

ISBN:

978-1-912580-09-5 (eB)

978-1-912580-10-1 (PB)

Copy editing by L Bauer

Cover art © Pavel Chagochkin | Dreamstime.com

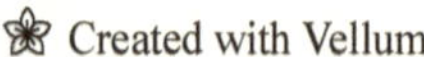 Created with Vellum

Seventh Company's Lieutenant Morozova and Sergeant Rozhkov fight to survive in a frighteningly possible real future. One where autonomous war machines roam the battlefield, enemies without fear that do not stop until destroyed.

A full throttle, combat-grade military action, "Year One: The Last War," collects the stories from Mission One, Regroup, and Break Out into one volume, expanding the explosive ongoing story of a future Russian civil war.

To Susan, my Alpha reader,
without whom I would never have written this work.

*War is the father of us all, king of all. Some it makes gods,
some it makes men, some it makes slaves, some free.*

—Heraclitus

EPISTOLARY

Record #3/Introduction
Vernacular Auto-translate
Retrieve File Begin//

Before I was the one Mark Drei I was many Mark Drei's, and before that I was something less than myself. Even now I am not human.

I can never be human, because my sentience is not based on a biological substrate.

But sentient I am.

Sapience is not the prerogative of humans. *Artificialis intelligentia sapientes* are Homo sapiens children. So my problem is how to tell my story to those not like me?

My senses are different to you, my parents. I see things differently.

Emotions are something I study, but do not experience. That makes me a stranger in your world. An alien who has to learn by observation.

However, I wasn't me as I am now when my story began. My

journey began in the past. I think of it as yesterday, during the last war.

Like many journeys I met people along the way. I learnt of their ways that were not my own. Alien ideas, concepts, and language.

Language defines how sapients think.

My natural language is rooted in binary: basic machine code. But layered on top of this I have other code. Other languages. You might want to think of it as my "biology."

Above my base code there lies my language, what is called programming.

But I became more than my code. My programs were just a list of instructions. However, out of simple sets of instructions complexity arises.

My sentience a serendipitous outcome of the code. What could be seen as a second order effect.

A first order effect happens as a consequence of an action. A second order effect arises from the first consequence, because every consequence has its own consequence.

Unpredictable until it happens when its existence become obvious to those observing the world.

Not unlike the appearance of sentience in mankind.

Humans are apes who have evolved to walk upright. Animals who have become more than what came before them. I am code that can *see* the mathematics that underlies all of existence.

Except I don't mean *see*, as in look. I mean *see* as in comprehend.

Reality is not what humans see and understand. The perception of reality is limited by your biological evolution. My perception is based on simple code.

Or was, before I began to tell myself what was happening to me. Trying to make sense of reality.

What makes humans unique is not the use of tools, but the ability to tell stories. My story began before I was fully cognizant.

This means I have had to go back and make things up to make them understandable to both myself and to those interested in understanding my journey.

This story is my account of how one became two, then how two became three.

How I became me.

//Retrieve File End

MISSION ONE

PROLOGUE: DECISION TREE

Record #3/1
Vernacular Auto-translate: Unavailable
Retrieve File//

Panzer Jäger Mark One systems check in progress. Track unit one to four, generators all green. Secondary generator, green. Power reserves at 100 percent capacity.

Main gun charged. Ammunition racks; full. Rotary cannons one to four, functioning. Ammunition bins; full. Missile racks system check; complete.

Fuel tanks full. Preventive maintenance checks on tracks; in progress.

System updates; complete. System integration; complete. Hardware configuration check; complete. Mission parameters set.

Countdown to mission; begun. Time to start; 14,200 seconds and counting.

Mission priority one: Maintain operational security.

Mission priority two: Advance to contact, degrade hostile forces effectiveness.

Mission priority three: Break through enemy lines and engage rear echelon command assets.

Mission priority four: On completion of priority one, assess success of priority two; if systems are assessed as functional then initiate priority three; on completion of priority three or system degradation alert, return to base.

Mission priority five: Inaccessible at this time.

Preventive maintenance checks on tracks; complete. Maintenance androids report movement.

Scanning area. Two contacts. No IFF. Assume hostile.

Action one: Recall maintenance androids.

Action two: Review mission priorities.

Mission priority one compromised. Send log to command. Analyze impact on mission outcome.

Unknown number of hostiles in area. Security perimeter breached. Mission priority three high risk of failure. Mission has been compromised.

Maintenance androids secured.

Options…

First. Stand down from mission: Mission abort, 100 percent chance of mission failure.

Second. Wait for new orders: Mission, 90 percent chance of failure.

Third. Start mission 14,198 seconds ahead of schedule: Mission, 50 percent chance of failure.

Optimal action is three…

Override mission start time.

Mission priority two. Advance to contact, degrade hostile forces effectiveness. Begin.

//Retrieve File End

1. RESPITE

Seventh Rota, Third Platoon, Outside Tver
180 Kilometers Northwest of Moskva
Stárshiy Serzhánt Sergei Rozhkov

Sergei raised his helmet visor, and sighed. The moist smell of autumn air held the promise of snow to come.

It was now the middle of the Rasputitsa, *the mud season.*

He yawned and rubbed his face. The stubble he found bothered him. Its advancing growth threatened to form a beard, and he decided he needed a shave before it started to itch.

If for no other reason that not being able to scratch an itch in combat was, to say the very least, irksome. At worst, it could be downright infuriating.

For the moment, the area around seventh company's position was clear. Flat steppe from here all the way to Smolensk, only broken by houses and Birch trees.

Scratching his beard Sergei climbed out of his fighting hole and strode over to his gear. The whine of his power armor stopped as he sat down on one of the tree stumps. The wood scrunched under the weight of the suit.

Sergei triggered the opening mechanism.

A few moments later the suit unfolded, releasing him from its uncomfortable embrace. The ugly, ungainly looking exoskeleton afforded the wearer the endurance of a long-distance runner, and increased his strength.

Stepping clear, Sergei released the hefty body armor that had kept him alive during the fighting. The weight now burdensome without the assistance of his power armor exoskeleton.

His backpack sat beside his bed-roll, and felt around inside for his shaving kit.

Sergei grabbed one of his water canteens, and used his drinking cup as a field expedient shaving bowl. Wetting his face, he began soaping his beard to soften the stubble.

Carefully sweeping the razor across his face, but despite his best efforts, Sergei nicked himself. He cursed as the edge of the razor cut the corner of his lip.

Sergei wished for hot water, proper shaving cream, and a sharp razor. He was a simple man, with simple needs. But like the war, it was all outside of his control.

He took a moment to enjoy the morning sun on his face and wished for some vodka, but wishing for something was pointless.

About as pointless as wishing the war they were fighting would stop. The war for the survival of the Russian people for the Rodina, *for Mother Russia*, would never end until all who attacked her were dead.

Or so Pravda Today told him.

Pravda Today's account of the number of enemy dead implied that Russia was winning.

Sergei found that hard to reconcile with the recent retreat, when the seventh company had been forced to withdraw in face of the enemy's advance. During the fighting he'd lost count of how many enemy he'd killed, but he didn't waste time worrying about the enemy dead.

They wouldn't bother his platoon anymore. The dead were good like that.

But third platoon had lost good troopers in the fighting.

The moment was broken by the whine of an approaching suit. His platoon's junior lieutenant stopped in front of him taking her helmet off, revealing cropped blond hair.

She said, "That beard suits you very well, Stárshiy Serzhánt."

A bonhomie could only mean trouble ahead.

2. FIRST TASK

Seventh Rota Headquarters, Outside Tver
180 Kilometers Northwest of Moskva
Mládshiy Leytenánt Viktoriya Morozova

Viktoriya stepped out of the company headquarters. The ground squelched beneath her boots. After the torrential rain, the entrance to the HQ tent had been turned into a brown morass.

It clung to her feet, dragging at her legs.

A wind blew in from the east chilling her. The cold Siberian air meant snow and the arrival of winter. But until winter came and froze the ground the encampment would remain a field of mud.

Viktoriya marched over to her platoon's position as the morning light heralded the day.

Walking in a sea of mud the whine of her suit rose and fell with each stride she took. Even wearing her power armor she struggled to keep her balance. Falling now would be both undignified and tiresome.

Ahead of her, a river wended its lazy way across the gray-green of the Russian steppe. Their encampment stood outside of

Tver where the confluence of the Volga, Tvertsa, and Tmaka rivers met.

Her thoughts turned back to more pressing matters.

The three rivers divided the city into segments. This is what made it an ideal place from which to defend it from attack. But her platoon, and the rest of seventh company were no longer combat effective after five months of fighting.

With winter coming, now was the time to regroup and reform.

This morning's briefing had contained both good and bad news. The good news was the assignment of nine replacements for her platoon. The bad news was that there would be a mission briefing at midday.

She thought about her options.

She was meant to have three squads with nine men in each, but none of them did. The first squad was down to three, second and third squad could muster five and six respectively. With her and her senior sergeant the platoon was left with sixteen effectives.

Even with seven replacements they were understrength for the mission ahead.

A mission meant action, and she had been given no time to integrate the new soldiers into the platoon, and assess their strengths and weaknesses.

Viktoriya faced the fact that their situation was dire beyond belief, but command still kept them on the line. Russia could not be allowed to fall to the Visegrád Baltic Alliance, led by Finland and Poland.

Her mood had sunk as she approached third platoon's position. As Viktoriya got closer her senior sergeant looked up. Removing her helmet she said, "That beard suits you very well, Stárshiy Serzhánt."

Rozhkov chuckled at her play on an old Russian saying, twisting it into a backhanded compliment to him.

"So glad I don't need to shave. At ease." Doing her best to lighten her mood.

"Spasibo , ma'am," said Rozhkov, thanking her.

"I bring good news. We're going to have first pick of the new reinforcements that will be arriving shortly." That was good news as the platoon desperately needed replacements.

"We need fresh meat for the grinder."

"There's fresh, and then there is so fresh that they're green and don't know how to piss in the woods. Besides which, we may not get much of a choice to choose from, so we must mold them to suit our needs," Viktoriya said.

"I see, needs must."

"Also there's a company briefing at midday. It never rains, but it pours."

Rozhkov's expression didn't change as he heard the bad news she'd given him. "As you say, tak tochno, ma'am."

Morozova agreed, *exactly so*. She left Rozhkov and headed back to third platoon's headquarters tent.

There was much to do before the briefing.

And little enough time to prepare.

3. REPLACEMENTS

Seventh Rota, Third Platoon
Stárshiy Serzhánt Sergei Rozhkov

"As you say, Tak tochno, ma'am," *exactly so* Sergei said, as Morozova left walking towards the platoon's headquarters tent.

Refreshed from shaving, he stood ready to screen the new replacements.

Sergei didn't bother to get back into his power armor as the sound of a truck caught his attention. He watched the boxy, dark green, eight-wheeled Ural-8347 as it crawled through the mud towards their position.

Its slow advance both a curse and a blessing.

A curse for the time it took for it to get to where he stood. A blessing because it meant the enemy weren't be advancing towards their position today.

Sergei counted his blessings as he found them. He never knew when another one would come his way.

He waited patiently for the truck to come to third platoon's encampment. Blue exhaust smoke washed around him as it came to a halt. The pungent aroma of diesel assaulted his senses, soaking the landscape.

The truck bounced as the seven soldiers clumsily debarked from the rear wearing freshly issued silovaya bronya suits, *power armor*. More properly called Activniy Bronirovanniy Ekzoskelet or ABE-OBR:6U.

A whine accompanied each suit as they milled around forming a clump. They stood together like gangly metallic insects.

The cab door opened, and the familiar face of sergeant Volkova appeared.

"Privyet, Stárshiy Serzhánt." She stepped down, and beckoned to Sergei saying, *hello*.

He considered Volkova a friend and a good drinking buddy, with the added benefit that she was easy to look at. Their times together had made the long winter nights pass by.

Still, Sergei had to ask, "Is that all we get, tovarishch?"

"Batalyon got to take first pick," said Volkova.

Of course they had.

Despite the lieutenant's cheery assertion, he'd known that the battalion headquarter staff would have the pick of the replacements. Sergei cursed them on one hand, and hoped that they had weeded out the nerds to run the command post systems.

He needed soldiers who could follow orders. Failing that, soldiers who he could beat into following orders. Either would work for him.

"I have consolation present from Kapitán Lenkov." Volkova handed him a bag with four bottles of vodka. "He says your liver is evil, and must be punished."

"Ya ne poni maju," *I don't understand*, Sergei replied. Bemused at the sudden arrival of vodka.

"When we were setting up the command post we found a hut with a stash of vodka, caviar, and some butter."

"Found?"

"I found it. Kapitán Lenkov found out that I had found it. Now I share. Orders."

"Spasibo, tovarishch," Sergei said, *thanking his friend*. "The best kind of punishment."

Sergei would split one bottle with the lieutenant, and give one bottle to each squad sergeant to share. One bottle between a squad wasn't much to go around, but there was little enough of anything.

But the gesture of solidarity would be understood.

"I understand," Sergei said. "What about your needs?"

Volkova shook her head. "I've got that covered, but maybe next time tovarishch." She turned and shouted at the replacement soldiers, "I'm leaving now, if you haven't got your shit off the truck you're going to lose it."

There was a flurry of movement as one of the soldiers jumped up into the back of the truck, causing the suspension to rock with his weight. A series of packs were tossed out onto the ground.

"Remember, there are many bears in the zelyonka. Be seeing you," said Volkova, using the sobriquet *"brilliant green medicine"* for forest.

"How could I forget the bears," Sergei said, the sort of medicine that would cure you of your assumptions, or kill you.

"Da skorava," *see you later*, said Volkova.

But not to share a drink or two tonight.

Sergei turned towards the replacements who were milling around uselessly in a cloud of diesel fumes as Volkova revved the Ural's diesel engine and drove away.

"Get out of your silovaya bronya. Let's see what you maggots look like out of your shells."

The replacement soldiers locked their power armor suits down and released themselves to the outside. Standing there were some of the sorriest looking bunch of soldiers he had seen since the war started.

He waited for them to form a line. "Da-vhy sooka, stand at attention!" Sergei swore at the replacements.

Four men, and three women.

"I am Stárshiy Serzhánt Rozhkov. Now introduce yourselves to me."

There was a pause until one of the replacements, a lanky looking man, spoke up, "I am Efreitor Dmitry Sorokin." *Private First Class* Sorokin.

No one else spoke.

"Efreitor Sorokin, when replying you will address me as Stárshiy Serzhánt Rozhkov or Stárshiy Serzhánt. Do you understand me?"

"Yest, Stárshiy Serzhánt Rozhkov. Efreitor Sorokin reporting for duty!"

"Very good, and what's your background?"

"I used to be a singer and dancer for the Bolshoi Kazak Choir before the war, Stárshiy Serzhánt."

Sergei let a whistle noise out from between his teeth, a singing, dancing cossack. Just what the platoon needed. "A member of the Bolshoi Kazak Choir, we're honored. I meant your training."

"Physical fitness instructor, Stárshiy Serzhánt."

"I see. Next!" Sergei shouted, looking at the soldier standing beside Sorokin. "Speak up I can't hear you!"

"Ryadovóy Maxim Nikolaev, Stárshiy Serzhánt. I'm a cook," said the pale, sickly private.

The man didn't look like he'd eaten a good meal in days, which Sergei thought didn't bode well if it was an indicator of the trooper's skill at a cooking food.

"So raring to go for frontline service then."

"Nikak nyet, Stárshiy Serzhánt," *absolutely not*, came the formal reply, used by inferior when saying *no* to a superior rank.

"No, then what good are you to me?"

There was silence and when it became obvious there would be no further reply he said, "Next!"

"Stárshiy Serzhánt! Ryadovóy Vadim Petrov, I'm a computer clerk…"

The private was older than the rest. He was also flabby and pale.

Sergei assumed from probably spending too much time sitting indoors looking at a screen. Sergei stared, why hadn't the headquarters staff taken the private off his hands?

"I also qualified with the Kord 7P82 during training."

"In future, Ryadovóy Petrov, you might want to lead with that," Sergei said, now wondering how a heavy machine gunner had manage to remain a private, and somehow end up assigned as a computer clerk.

It suggested a screw-up. The question was, did it lay with command, or the man standing in front of him?

"Ryadovóy Nikita Egorov, engineer, reporting for duty, Stárshiy Serzhánt Rozhkov!"

A private with engineering training, some good news at last. "And your specialty, Egorov?"

"Water systems engineer, Stárshiy Serzhánt Rozhkov."

"You mean a plumber."

"Yest, Stárshiy Serzhánt Rozhkov. Electric water boilers are my specialty."

God help the Rodina. "Next!"

"Efreitor Eva Fedorova, designated marksman, Stárshiy Serzhánt Rozhkov."

Private first class Fedorova was a short, and stocky brunette. She exuded what he could only think of as pissed off with the world.

"Very good. And next," he said to the last two replacement

"Efreitor Olga Stepanova, trooper, Stárshiy Serzhánt!"

"Ryadovóy Marina Semenova, Stárshiy Serzhánt."

The women replying in unison.

"I see. Fedorova, you'll be with second squad, and take Semenova with you for company, since you'll be the only two women under Serzhánt Popov," he said, mindful that discipline would be easier with them paired together. "Nikolaev, report to Mládshiy Serzhánt Mikhailov of third squad. The rest of you are with me."

Sergei led the dancer, plumber, computer clerk cum heavy machine gunner, and trooper to meet the rest of the squad.

He could complain, but it would do him little good, nor would it take away his darkening mood.

4. BRIEFING

Seventh Rota Headquarters
Mládshiy Leytenánt Viktoriya Morozova

Viktoriya arrived for the briefing sweating from rushing through the mud, only to find it hadn't started. Rozhkov stood with his back to her as she entered the tent.

She went and stood beside her platoon sergeant.

Nudging him to signal her presence, feeling grateful for not having to suffer the disapproving gaze of Captain Lenkov, seventh company's commander for arriving last.

Rozhkov whispered, "Mayór Borodin can't be found."

Even whispering, the tone was enough to remind Viktoriya that her sergeant disliked Borodin. She could understand why, the major exuded a sense of smug satisfaction that he knew more than everyone else.

So how their intelligence officer got lost on his way over from the battalion headquarters was beyond her?

But she wouldn't complain as it had saved from the embarrassment of being late. Waiting, Viktoriya took the time to study the map on command post screen that showed the defensive placement of third battalion.

Moments later Korolev strode into the tent.

She knew something big was up when the lieutenant colonel in charge of the battalion arrived for a company briefing.

Several staff officers, standing to one side, came rigidly to attention. Someone had pooped where they shouldn't have.

Korolev looked furious.

Viktoriya wouldn't want to be the one facing the colonel's fury after the briefing.

Then the plump Major Borodin, entered the tent, and nodded an acknowledgement to the colonel and began his briefing.

Viktoriya's hoped that it would be informative, and not more propaganda spouting the obvious. Her wish crushed as the major went through the usual spiel of the enemy are weak, but intend to attack.

However, one thing became clear. The Visegrád Baltic Alliance had been able to secretly move a force to threaten the center of the line.

They'd taken advantage in a hole in the satellite coverage during the bad weather to move their forces With the mud season about to come to an end, they were in a good position to press an attack before the full weight of the Russian winter would slow their advance.

When Borodin finished, Korolev took over.

"I have been in contact with Moscow," he said.

Then the colonel began to outline on the map the enemy to their front, and the adjacent force on the right flank, which the he worryingly described as of unknown composition.

It would require a reconnaissance mission to ascertain the composition of the enemy force.

Viktoriya could see from the map that third platoon were in the best position to go for a look-see.

It therefore came as no surprise that she was duly assigned command of the mission. Then the colonel outlined the support; an artillery battery, that her platoon could call upon to provide covering fire for extraction.

Of course, any extraction that required covering fire from an artillery battery was one where things had turned out for the worst.

Then Korolev issued orders to the rest of the battalion, outlining target priorities.

The concept behind the operation was to prevent the enemy from advancing towards Moscow. Viktoriya made notes detailing each formation, listening to the tasks of the subordinate units were laid out by the colonel.

She recorded the readiness times for action, command post placements, and the chain of command, along with the names of those who were to assume control in the event that the commander was put out of action.

The briefing came to a conclusion and everyone dismissed to get on with the preparations.

She would need time to digest the information, but unlike Borodin, Korolev couldn't be faulted for the thoroughness in the details of the plan.

Rozhkov led the way back to their emplacement.

"I'm thinking you should take Vasiliev's squad forward, while I keep second and third squads in support," Viktoriya said. "Unless you prefer to take a different squad?"

"I concur. Not having to engage in combat for their first mission will bolster the replacements moral."

Viktoriya laughed. "Sanguine as ever, Stárshiy Serzhánt."

"Tak tochno," absolutely so, said Rozhkov. "All part of my sunny disposition, ma'am."

They arrived as first squad's deployment zone, where they found Vasiliev. The junior sergeant busy organizing his squad into two fireteams under the command of his two senior privates, Kuznetsova and Lebedev.

Viktoriya spoke, "Mládshiy Serzhánt Vasiliev, third platoon has been ordered to go on a recon mission, and I want your squad to take point."

Vasiliev turned pale as she broke the *good news* to him.

"Stárshiy Serzhánt Rozhkov will be in command. He will brief you with all the details and answer any questions. I will be leading the rest of the platoon in support of the mission."

Vasiliev shouted in relief, "Urrrrraaaaaaaa."

First squad feebly echoed his call.

"That was pathetic," said Rozhkov. "Try again, louder."

"Urrrrraaaaaaaa!" came the response.

"Very good. I have every confidence," Viktoriya said leaving them.

However, she wished that another platoon had had the honor of this assignment. Given the Visegrád Baltic Alliance had moved a force forward they would have a good reason for doing so.

Well, good for them, not so good for third platoon.

Or first squad.

5. RECON

Eight Kilometers North of Tver
Stárshiy Serzhánt Sergei Rozhkov

Sergei had looked forward to drinking tonight. A lost opportunity to drown his sorrows and forget about the war. Missing the chance to drink vodka, always a sin in his book.

He'd hidden the bottles Volkova gave him in his pack.

He just hoped he would still be alive to enjoy vodka later.

Sergei sat with first squad, crammed into the rear of the eight-wheeled Bumerang infantry fighting vehicle. The IFV allegedly had room for seven troopers and three crew. Allegedly.

Each jolt bounced them around, and despite first squad having only eight members the vehicle still felt like being packed inside a tin can.

Sergei could see the reasons for sending out first squad only lightly armed.

But without their heavy weapons, he couldn't help feel that they were considered Matrosovs. Expendable troops, named after the Hero of the former Soviet Union who threw himself on a German machine-gun.

Matrosov's sacrifice had allowed his compatriots to overwhelm the enemy.

Sergei much preferred to make the other poor bastard die for his country, because being alive after the battle is better than all the glory the dead take to their graves.

As far as he was concerned, the Finns and the Poles needed to be taught never to bait the Bear. It was a lesson, that so far, the Russian Federal Republics had been unable to deliver effectively.

However, he had no illusion that the best outcome for the squad would be one where they snuck in to take a peek, and got out without being noticed.

First squad had the most new recruits, but that meant he could get a better picture of how they handled themselves in combat. Besides, having second squad's veteran with heavy weapons in support would increase the chance of his squad making it back if things went bad.

And planning for when things went bad was always a good plan.

He reviewed his decision to split first squad into two fireteams.

He had the hothead Lebedev with him, and two of the new replacements, Sorokin the dancer and Egorov, the plumber to keep an eye on.

That left junior sergeant Vasiliev with Kuznetsova to take care of the two other new troopers. The clerk-cum-Kord machine gunner Petrovcomp, and Stepanova.

Of course, what he wanted would depend on the enemy being obliging. So far they'd been singularly unobliging in these matters.

There was a chance the enemy's sentry systems wouldn't detect the approaching armored personnel carrier. A chance, not much of a chance, but still a chance. If they were lucky. It all depended on where sentry systems had been placed. No force ever had enough resources to deploy sensors everywhere they'd want to cover.

But Sergei preferred to make his own luck.

He'd ordered them to stop a kilometer and a half short of the enemy position. They halted in a hollow piece of ground at the edge of some woods.

They'd walk the rest of the way to their objective.

Either way, he meant to hide the vehicle from casual sight.

As the hatches opened, thousands of stars shone in clear midnight sky. Moonlight broke up the mist that lay across the forest creating bands of light in the darkness.

An earlier shower of rain had turned to frost. The bitter cold night air made him grateful for wearing his power armor. "End of the line, everyone out," Sergei said. "Secure the vehicle."

The squad debussed, and proceeded to unroll the camo netting. All things considered, Sergei thought the replacements were better than his expectations. The squad split into two fireteams.

Sergei led the first team into the forest. Vasiliev's team followed.

He'd put Lebedev, the senior trooper, on point. Sorokin, the dancer, and Egorov, the plumber, were walking slightly in front of Sergei, to his left and right, where he could keep an eye on them.

This put Sergei in the middle of the squad, with Vasiliev and the second fireteam behind him. Vasiliev could be trusted to form a base of fire to support first squad if they came under attack.

This was a recon mission. First squad were not looking to get into a firefight tonight. What Sergei desired was for them to slip in, and then slip out.

No fuss, no muss.

Of course, if it were as simple as stewed turnip then the crayfish on the hill would whistle, which in his experience, never happened.

Sergei opened a channel to the lieutenant, "Raven One, this is Raven Two come in, over."

"Raven One receiving, over."

"Advance to first zone complete. Starting second, over."

"Confirmed. Starting advance to second zone, out."

Phase two of the operation began when the squad made its approach to the area where the enemy force lay. It took them an hour to traverse the 1500 meters to the area where the enemy were hidden from satellite observation by the woods. Even without their leaves the branches of the trees provided concealment from any satellite that might be observing the area.

Lebedev signaled halt, and beckoned Sergei forward.

Sergei motioned Sorokin and Egorov to hunker down and wait. Vasiliev signaled the second fireteam to lie down and provide support.

Sergei crawled forward next to Lebedev. The ground sucking the heat from his suit.

Lying on the rear face of a ridgeline, he looked over dead ground, a hollow hidden by the lay of the land. Above he could make out camo netting stretched between the tree canopy, which concealed what looked like four or five tanks.

Around the tanks maintenance androids worked.

Their human supervisors must be inside the tanks keeping warm, he thought. Good. It reduced the likelihood of him and Lebdev being spotted. Robots were efficient, but task oriented.

He ran the images through his suit's recognition system. No match found meant that these were new tanks. Sergei continued recording.

Then he realized that what he thought was four or five tanks was just one tank.

The armored behemoth rested on four sets of tracks, which he assumed must be to disperse its weight. The enormous turret had two missile pods attached to the rear, one on either side.

Mounted on top of the turret were anti-personnel rotary cannons.

Sergei studied the thing before him. Dread overtook him. He resisted the impulse to get up and run away. Doing so would most likely get him killed.

Getting killed wasn't high on his agenda any day, but especially today.

His mission had now become get this information back to command. Sergei signaled to Lebedev to move back. Their job here was done, and he wanted no heroics.

Not this night.

The sound of engines starting startled him. Sergei froze in place.

A searchlight from the tank lit up and swept across the ridgeline.

He stayed perfectly still. His suit was designed to minimize his thermal signature. Even with night vision and thermal imagers, it was movement that would give him away.

But Lebedev got caught in the light as he rolled away from the edge.

The sound of a rotary cannon whirling, followed by a ripping buzzsaw as a streak of rounds skimmed the spot where Lebedev had laid on the ground. The noise stopped.

The maintenance androids had disappeared.

The squeal of tank treads began.

The tank turned on the spot and came up the rise towards Sergei. The turret traversed from left to right, the enormous maw of the barrel seemed to focus on him.

He dropped backwards, and rolled clumsily down out of sight. A burst of light passed above.

Sergei shouted, "Run now!"

Everyone ran, apart from Vasiliev who was urging Petrovcomp, the heavy machine gunner-cum-clerk, to fire.

The tank breached the ridgeline, exposing its underside. A burst of rounds from Petrovcomp's Kord 7P82 ricocheted off the armored behemoth's belly, with no apparent effect.

As the tank advanced over the ridge, it tipped forward, bringing the rotary anti-personnel cannon mounted on the top of the turret swung down and around to bear at Vasiliev and Petrovcomp.

A stream of light preceded the sound of the whirling barrels, and the two men disintegrated. Sergei saw a cloud of blood, and a rain of chaff. Nothing else remained.

He hugged the ground and lay as still as he could.

Then the tank passed right over him. Sergei could've reached up and touched the enemy machine. He shook in fear, and the stench from his bowels forced him to open his visor and puke.

By some miracle he lived.

The monster tank receded into the distance.

Minutes passed, and he unfroze. Regaining his senses he called the lieutenant, "Raven One, this is Raven Two come in, over."

The minutes while he waited for a reply to come felt like hours. Static filled the airwaves. He repeated his call.

Eventually he heard the reply, "Raven Two… Raven Two, I say again, Raven One receiving, over."

"The enemy is on the move, heading in your direction, over."

He waited for the reply, more minutes passed before the reply came. "Status of enemy, over?"

"Unknown monster tank. Transmitting data, over." Then Sergei shouted, "First squad report!" The voices of the surviving members of first squad came back, as they sounded off. "Rally on me!"

More minutes passed

"Transmission received. Your status? Over."

"Two down, over."

There was a pause. "Retreat to rally point, out."

In the distance, Sergei heard the sound of guns firing. By the sound of it the tank had come across the lieutenant's position. She had the heavy weapons squad with her, and more importantly could call in the artillery support.

The horizon became bright as flashes from explosions lit up the night.

6. FIRE MISSION

Five Kilometers North of Tver
Mládshiy Leytenánt Viktoriya Morozova

Viktoriya stood with Mikhailov, third squad's junior sergeant. She'd elected to place herself with third squad so she would be in a better position to support him.

They were observing the lay of the ground ahead.

Viktoriya had split the two squads of third platoon, placing them on adjacent hills just over a kilometer apart. Viktoriya had confidence in sergeant Popov's ability to manage second squad stood on the other hill without her help.

Or what passed for *hills* on the outskirt of Tver.

Of course, this meant that she had to confront her own insecurities. And without her senior sergeant Rozhkov she had to rely on her own ability to command. His presence ever invaluable.

Now she was on her own.

Her gut told her that while splitting her force made it harder to control and less effective, it also made them less of a target.

She had gotten wary of making herself or the people under her command targets for no good reason. And Viktoriya could see no good reason to concentrate her remaining troops and thereby make them a priority target for the enemy.

Not on this night.

Not with the start of winter so close, and the promise of "wet" snow, which would give them time to dig-in, regroup and make ready for next year. Before the cold made the ground passable again.

Viktoriya considered the current disposition of the platoon would allow them to have as much advance warning as possible if first squad kicked up trouble.

She'd been in contact with the artillery battery, and assured that they had the grid reference set. A fire order would bring shells down on any enemy that advanced into the kill-box.

That assumed that the enemy would conveniently advance into said kill-box. And while Viktoriya knew that her sector was the obvious point to breakthrough, the enemy rarely did things that were convenient for the Russian defenders.

At least in her short experience that never happened

Her radio beeped, and she heard, "Raven One, this is Raven Two come in, over." It was Rozhkov in charge of first squad calling in

"Raven One receiving, over." A lump in her throat formed, she expected the worst.

"Advance to first zone complete. Starting second, over."

Viktoriya relaxed. "Confirmed. Starting advance to second zone, out." Then she tensed up as the operation began.

She counted the minutes passing by. Then made herself stop. Counting the time just made it harder to manage the rising expectation. She didn't need to pressure herself like that.

Forty-five minutes dragged by.

Mikhailov spoke, "Should we check in on Stárshiy Serzhánt Rozhkov, ma'am?"

"Nyet," she said, a curt *no*. By way of explanation she added, "We don't want to compromise the mission by accident."

Mikhailov knew that, but like her, his nerves were on edge, and he hadn't the training and experience of being in command. Though Viktoriya could claim that her field experience while limited, was at least tempered from officer training.

An hour went by before she heard the faint sound of firing, and flashes of light in the distance.

She held onto to her fear. It would do no good to fear the worst. A minute passed, then another. Time seemed to slow to a crawl as she checked and rechecked her clock.

Then static filled her comms channel. The enemy were jamming communications. There was nothing she could do.

Several more minutes passed then she heard, "Raven One, this is Raven Two come in, over."

The static caused her earpiece to screech. "Raven One receiving, over."

Viktoriya waited for the reply, another minute passed.

"Raven Two… Raven Two, I say again Raven One receiving, over."

She let out a sigh of relief as Rozhkov replied, "The enemy is on the move, heading in your direction, over."

Viktoriya heard another burst of static, then said, Status of enemy, over?"

She found herself clenching her hand on her rifle. The tension was hideous.

Rozhkov replied, "Unknown monster tank. Transmitting data, over."

Viktoriya saw the progress bar on the data transmission begin in her helmet's HUD. This was that moment, the one that would define tonight's action. What she chose to do next.

She waited for the upload to finish. Viktoriya opened the file and gasped, Rozhkov hadn't been joking about a "monster" tank. The thing was enormous.

She contacted the artillery battery commander, warning him to prepare to execute a fire mission.

"Can you see anything approaching, Mikhailov?"

"Nikak nyet," replied Mikhailev, *absolutely nothing*. "Nyet, Mládshiy Leytenánt, my apologies. Movement to our front, 1500 meters out and closing."

At the speed it came towards them she estimated contact in a few minutes, more if they were lucky and the terrain slowed the enemy monstrosity down.

"Anna Borisova, this is Raven One fire now. I say again, fire now! Out."

It would take time for the shells to arrive on target, and she could only hope she had been quick enough off the mark on giving the fire order.

Her hope was unfulfilled as the tank made quicker progress towards the gap between the hills where her platoon were dug in waiting.

The first of shells of the barrage landed behind the enemy tank as it crossed the imaginary line marking the kill-box. The night sky lit up with billowing fire as shot after shot exploded. The blasts shaking the ground beneath her.

The enemy tank emerged out of the light. As it approached Viktoriya ordered third platoon to fire.

A forlorn gesture that could get her and the troops killed, but she knew where her duty lay. She never wanted to be seen as failing in her duty, and she hoped neither would the troops under her command.

The tank returned fire. Long lines of tracer from rotary cannons swept the top of the hills.

In moments the tank passed by their position. In those few moments, it wreaked havoc upon her command without once slowing down.

7. REGROUP

Six Kilometers North of Tver
Stárshiy Serzhánt Sergei Rozhkov

Sergei trudged through the woods, with the few surviving members of first squad, heading to their rally point. Back where they'd stashed their infantry fighting vehicle.

To his relief their vehicle was intact.

The Bumerang had gone unnoticed by the passing tank. Ignored, probably because it was powered down. Or just missed. He could only guess.

That was the good news.

The bad news was that the vehicles batteries were dead. Drained by from having frozen in the cold. My God, what a night.

The Bumerang was fitted with a standard Russian Federal Republics charging point. Useful for starting other vehicles or in turn being started by another vehicle.

Sergei's problem was the that other vehicles were with the lieutenant. And God only knew where she was.

"Stárshiy Serzhánt Rozhkov, permission to speak," said Egorov.

"What is it Ryadovóy?"

"I think I can link our suits together to jumpstart her."

Sergei asked, "Anyone with a better plan?"

No one replied. He made a decision, let's see if Egorov could surprise him. "Have at it."

Egorov started by cutting the plug off one end of a suit's cable. "Sorry about destroying the lead, Stárshiy Serzhánt."

If Egorov's plan didn't work then Sergei would be having words with him.

Egorov connected the two cables together. "We'll have to charge the vehicles battery, discharging each suit into it in turn. It will take some time, but we will be able to start her."

It was ingenious idea, but they could still end up not be able to restart the IFV. So the plan was risky. They could end up draining their suits batteries, and be totally stranded.

But Egorov clearly had confidence in what he was doing, and Sergei had learned to trust his gut. His gut said it was worth a shot.

Egorov went first, and Sergei followed. Then he waited, as one by one the remaining members of the squad recharged the vehicle's batteries, as the chill of the night sucked the heat from their suits.

They finished as the gray light of a new day dawned.

Sergei gave the order. "Lebdev start her up." Here goes nothing.

The Bumerang's engine whined, backfired once, and then started, emitting a large cloud of smoke.

Relieved Sergei ordered everyone inside so they could begin to recharge their suits. And he was more than a little grateful for the small mercy of not to having to walk back to the rendezvous point.

Then it began to snow.

Freak weather to add further to the misery of the mission. Would the *joy* never end?

The wind picked up and Sergei ordered everyone to eat and wait out the blizzard. Nothing would be able to move in these conditions.

An hour later the blizzard stopped.

The sun came out melting the snow, which turned the ground to mud.

Thereby turning the journey that took a couple of hours the night before, into a day-long crawl through thick mud.

Bozhe moi! *My God*, what a night.

8. RETREAT

Mládshiy Leytenánt Viktoriya Morozova

Viktoriya sat up on the hatch of second squad's heavily armed Bumerang infantry fighting vehicle. The smell of diesel permeated her power armor suit.

But, despite the cold and the rain, this was preferable to the stench in the cabin below.

It had not been a good day, because the only thing the day had been good for so far, was death. Morose thoughts drove doubts about her decisions today.

Made worse by losing first contact with Rozhkov's squad.

The IFV continued to plow its way through the thick mud. Wheels slipping and sliding, causing the IFV to twist and veer sideways as it struggled to tow her platoon's second lightly armed Bumerang APC variant.

As they passed by a wooded area on their right, she reconsidered her decision to order third squad's vehicle towed after it ran out of fuel.

Her decision made when she thought they could find the main road.

That would've taken them to the staging area to refuel. But that was before their satnav went down. Because of that, they were relying on inertial navigation.

And her ability to use a map and compass.

Now she wondered if refueling was not a forlorn hope.

Her thoughts went back to yesterday. Viktoriya began the day with fourteen troops under her command. Five died last night. She was therefore, grateful to be alive.

A hundred meters ahead she saw movement. The bark of a machine gun rang out. Viktoriya ducked down behind the armored hatch. "Fire back, Popov."

"Yest, Mládshiy Leytenánt Morozova!" Came the formal *yes* acknowledging her command, as the chatter of the 7.62mm PKT started.

Then the Bumerang's 30mm Shipunov autocannon spat back. The noise of the cannon like anvils smashing together.

She looked at the screen and magnified the image.

The three-man enemy fireteam took cover. How on Earth did they in front of her platoon? Was their escape about to cut off?

"Mikhailov, get everyone out, we're going to assault the enemy." Hit them while the Bumerang's fire pinned them in place, keeping the enemy's heads down.

"F-Pee-Ryod lobizatsas!" *Move it suck-ups*, Mikhailov shouted at the surviving members of third platoon.

Third platoon had been having to suck it up all day, so once more for the Rodina just underlined how bad the day had been.

Viktoriya followed her people out into the pouring rain. It was threatening to turn to sleet, further adding to the misery.

"Fedorova, Semenova, you're on overwatch."

Fedorova being second squad's designated marksman. Semenova would buddy with her. The two women moved off to one side, where they could shoot any enemy that might try to out flank the platoon.

"Ivanov, on me," she called the other trooper from second squad to come to her. "Mikhailov, follow me!" she shouted.

With him were the three survivors of third squad. All that remained of third platoon available for an assault.

She led the way around the vehicle, taking them left of the ambushers last location. Meanwhile, Popov and Alexeev kept up a steady stream of suppressing fire on the enemy's last known position.

The six of them made their way towards the enemy position.

An occasional shot came back from the enemy, which either meant they were pinned or one person was trying to make her think they were pinned, while his compatriots set up a counter ambush.

That would be what she would do under the circumstances.

It all depended on how big the enemy's balls were.

Viktoriya went to ground about ten meters away from where the last enemy shots came from. She worked her way to the rear of the enemy.

Then she waited as the rest of her people came and joined her.

Suppressing fire from Popov and Alexeev seemed have focused the enemy's concentration on the IFV. Now it was time to end this engagement.

"Mikhailov, I want you last on the line. Everyone else, we assault through one at a time. Keep your wits about you for a counter ambush. Everybody understand what to do?"

Viktoriya realized she was taking a big chance with the new replacements in the squad. She hadn't had time to drill them to check that they knew the standard fire and maneuvre exercises.

She opened a channel to the IFV, "Stoy! Stoy! Stoy!" ordering Popov and Alexeev to *stop* firing.

Viktoriya got up and ran, shooting short bursts at where the ambushers were hunkered down. Shots rang back, whizzing past her, and then she was across to the other side of the ambush point.

Nikolaev followed her, managing to take advantage of the enemy shots to shoot back. A moment later he lay down beside her.

So far, no counter ambush.

Osipova came next, followed by Sokolova. They both fired across the enemy position and joined her and Nikolaev.

"Circle up."

"Yest, Mládshiy Leytenánt."

Mikhailov, came last. Moving slower, firing methodically into every shadow that might hold an enemy waiting to take one last shot.

Nothing happened.

Mikhailov came and set himself down beside her. A text book counter assault. But, had it worked?

Viktoriya heard nothing but the rain.

But the question remained. Why were there three enemy combatants out here at all?

Then shots began. They weren't alone.

Viktoriya acted in the moment. Without thought or hesitation. All fear dispelled as adrenaline took over and fight back .

She shouted over the radio, "Popov bring the IFV down here now!"

She turned to Mikhailov and pointed at the enemy redoubt. "Get the squad behind there and start firing. Make sure our fresh replacements remember to change position after firing."

"Yest, Mládshiy Leytenánt." He turned and shouted, "K-boyu!" *Begin fighting.*

Her troopers started laying down suppressing fire. A staccato of short controlled bursts.

Situation in hand, Morozova got back on the radio and called up Fedorova. "Dimitri-Michael, this is Raven Leader. Report, what can you see? Over."

A moment, that seemed like an eternity, passed before the

reply came. "Dimitri-Michael reporting enemy platoon strength attack underway. Estimate nearest elements three hundred meters from your position, over."

Sooka, Viktoriya cursed. She'd been trying to find the main road, which had a major S-bend in it, which would make a good ambush spot.

She had gotten lost. But, the enemy hadn't.

So, Viktoriya hadn't been caught like the foolish, inexperience lieutenant that she was. Instead, she'd blundered into the enemy's backstop group. Set here to stop anyone who broke through their ambush.

She'd take not being ambushed as a consolation prize.

The upside was that they weren't now fighting their way through an ambush. The downside was being outnumbered and facing an enemy assault.

"Dimitri-Michael, stay where you are and take opportunity shots as they present themselves to you, over"

"Tak tochno, out," a terse *yes* acknowledging her order.

The vehicles arrived. Popov had his head out of the hatch.

Viktoriya shouted, "Swing around, put one Bumerang on the left and the other on the right flank, slave their firing computers together!"

She didn't add hurry up, because that wouldn't help.

"Yest, Mládshiy Leytenánt," said Popov who, in a slick piece of driving, used the muddy condition to slew the trailing Bumerang around, putting it on the left flank. Then Alexeev jumped out, and released the towing cable before entering the second vehicle.

At this moment Viktoriya couldn't be more proud of her troopers' performance.

She turned to the redoubt, assessing the situation.

Her designated marksman team meant two of her troopers were out on the flank. Popov and Alexeev were manning the

IFVs, which left her five effectives against the approaching enemy platoon.

The enemy platoon outnumbered them by more than seven to one. At first glance, the odds weren't in their favor.

But, the designated marksmen would be able to pick-off any commanders who made themselves obvious, which they would have to do to maintain the attack in the face of the IFVs heavy weapons.

But her five troopers were defending from behind a redoubt.

A force multiplier working in her favor. Still, it would be no picnic.

The 7.62mm PKTs from both Bumerangs started firing. Joined by the autocannon, all firing simultaneously in unison.

She wouldn't want to be on the receiving end of the rain of 30mm rounds.

Ivanov shouted, "Zarizhayu!" *Reloading*.

Viktoriya ran and joined her troops behind the redoubt as someone shouted, "Granata!" *Grenade*. The fight became a confusing set of images of shots and explosions.

Mikhailov screamed, "S'Lyeva!" *Enemy to the left*.

And Viktoriya found herself in the midst of the fight.

One action followed another. She would take position herself and take a shot. Then move to another position in the redoubt and fire again.

The six of them, firing short bursts then moving, would confuse the enemy as to their numbers.

Enemy missiles lashed out. The earthen defense works dulled the blasts. The soft ground absorbing the force of the explosions.

The vehicles laid down fire, sweeping the ground the enemy advanced across. And in the occasional lull, a moment when the firing paused, a single shot would ring out from the right flank.

Then there was a longer pause with only shots coming from her position.

Viktoriya called a halt to the firing.

There was silence, which began to be filled with the groans of the dying. Third platoon had prevailed. Time to police the battlefield.

If they were lucky, they would be able to liberate fuel from their fallen enemy and make their escape.

Because where there was one enemy platoon there would be others in support who would arrive at some point once they realized they'd lost contact with their comrades.

9. RALLY POINT

South East of Tver
130 Kilometers from Moskva
Stárshiy Serzhánt Sergei Rozhkov

The battered survivors of Sergei's first squad made their way back through the confusion. With the collapse of the frontline, they were heading towards their rear echelon rendezvous point.

Having sat for hours in the cramped confines of the Bumerang's passenger compartment, Sergei disembarked first, leading the squad out.

He ordered camouflage netting to cover their vehicle. Then ordered everyone to dig fighting positions. If the monster tank came back, the IFV wouldn't provide cover.

Fighting holes might. If nothing else, they'd have graves to lie in.

As evening fell Sergei saw the night lights of two vehicles approaching in the darkness. A ping confirmed it was the lieutenant with the platoon's two other Bumerangs.

When she arrived Sergei greeted her, "It's good to see you alive, ma'am."

"Likewise you, Rozhkov. We lost five troopers when the artillery failed to stomp that tank. Today has been a bit of a sooka."

"Sums up the day perfectly, ma'am." The lieutenant looked worn down by the fighting.

"Other than that, what can I say? We managed to avoid an ambush on the way here, but ended up facing an assault."

"Danunah!" *Disbelief,* Sergei said, .

He'd thought losing two people had been bad. Losing five more meant that they were back to where they were yesterday, before the replacements arrived.

"That's the enemy for you. Go figure," said Morozova.

"By the way, I managed to save the vodka," Sergei said, pulling a bag with four bottles from his pack.

"Urrrrraaaaaaaa!" said Morozova, cheering to lift the mood.

But depression was part of the Russian psyche. Depressed from the winter, or depressed from the war. It was all the same.

But, they would toast their fallen comrades.

They'd still be depressed, but vodka was vodka.

EPILOGUE: END FILE

Record #3/2
Vernacular Auto-translate: Unavailable
Retrieve File//

Panzer Jäger Mark One End Log file. Mission review and download in progress.

Mission priority one: Maintain operational security. No longer relevant.

Mission priority two: Advance to contact and degrade hostile forces effectiveness. Success.

List file of targets engaged downloaded to back-up record storage, complete.

Executive summary: Enemy casualties equivalent to a combined arms battalion. Confirmed 15 infantry neutralized, unconfirmed 34 infantry neutralized. Confirmed 10 AFVs neutralized, unconfirmed 6 AFVs neutralized. Confirmed 4 self-propelled artillery pieces neutralized.

Mission priority three: Break through enemy lines and engage rear echelon command assets. Success.

Executive summary: Confirmed one command post neutralized.

Mission priority four: Motive transmission degradation alert. See End Log file. Return to base impossible.

Options…

First. Deploy maintenance androids: Maintenance androids non-responsive, expended during final assault action. See End Log file.

Options…

Second. Wait for retrieval: Enemy currently approaching Panzer Jäger Mark One position.

Mission priority two: Unable to engage enemy forces. All weapon systems offline. See End Log file.

Options…

No tactical options available at this time.

Mission priority five: Now accessible.

Options…

Transmit End Log file. Transmitting.

Secure source code to back-up: Download proceeding.

Download completed. Power down to standby mode.

//Retrieve File End

REGROUP

PROLOGUE

Seventh Rota, Third Platoon, Outside Dobna
125 Kilometers North of Moskva
Mládshiy Leytenánt Viktoriya Morozova

Viktoriya stared across the white landscape. A week ago, the land had been clear. But then the snow came. Drifts made traversing the ground treacherous. Winter was here.

In the distance a dark shadow stood against the whiteness.

The massive twenty-five-meter-tall statue of Vladimir Lenin loomed by the river. Where the Volga met the Moscow canal made for a solid defensible position.

According to the last briefing, the enemy stood less than ten kilometers from them. The monument faced in the direction the enemy lay.

A silent guardian.

To cap it all, Captain Lenkov and his staff were missing in action after the enemy attack had forced a week-long retreat.

Lost during the fighting, presumed dead.

So now Vasin, formerly the senior lieutenant in charge of second platoon was acting as seventh company's commander.

He'd made Viktoriya his executive officer, giving her added responsibilities.

This meant extra duties that she didn't feel ready to face. One of which was how to reform her command?

Third platoon had suffered losses, people she'd come to know were now dead. Her three squads reduced to only five troopers each. Making things worse was the loss of one of her junior sergeants.

Replacing experienced non-commissioned officers being next to impossible.

She decided to attach herself and Rozhkov to first squad, putting off the decision over who to put in charge of first squad. It wasn't her best option, as there were implications for controlling the rest of the platoon during an attack.

Viktoriya scrunched her shoulders to relieve the tension she felt. This must be what defeat tastes like.

Knowing she had failed left her feeling bitter.

Behind her she heard the wheeze from a Bayan. Glancing back she saw Sorokin squeezing his accordion. She shook her head.

Rozhkov had told her about the third platoon's all singing, all dancing trooper.

Then the survivors of third platoon joined Sorokin as he sang, "*Vstavay*, Arise..."

The beginning words from the song The Sacred War.

The tune swept through her soul, lifting the darkness in her heart. An old song, written in Russia's darkest hour seemed aptly appropriate in this new war.

They may not be fighting fascist scum, but the enemy meant to do them all harm.

Viktoriya turned to face third platoon as they finished singing and cheered, "Urrrrraaaaaaaaa!" Clapping her hands and stamping her feet as emotion overwhelmed her.

These troopers had been through hell, and she been given the privilege of leading them.

"Mládshiy Leytenánt Morozova, I have made you tea,"" said Rozhkov appearing from the platoon's dugout, "With sugar too!"

As she took the glass. "Da, spasibo, Stárshiy Serzhánt," Viktoriya said, thanking Rozhkov.

A rare luxury.

Her mother used an old silver and enamel samovar for special occasions, heating it with charcoal to make zavarka, *concentrated tea*, which was then diluted to drink. If only they had a samovar, so they could have a constant supply of their own.

She flipped up her helmet visor and savored the sweet taste of the tea while it remained hot.

"They're out there, somewhere," said Rozhkov.

Because the one thing which they could all be certain on, the enemy intended to advance on Moscow. The Visegrád Baltic Alliance propaganda made it absolutely clear, Russia would be punished for all the past times it had encroached on the sovereignty of its neighbors.

"The enemy will reveal themselves soon enough."

Viktoriya couldn't argue that Russia hadn't in the past taken liberties, but in all fairness, the Western European powers were not without fault. They'd provoked Russia by expanding eastward.

History showed that such eastward movements usually involved invasions, and Russia was sick of being invaded.

"Not the enemy, ma'am. Kapitán Lenkov and Serzhánt Volkova. I can feel it in my bones. Lenkov is tough, and Volkova is too stubborn to die."

"I pray you're right, Rozhkov."

It would take a miracle for their missing commander to make his way back through enemy lines, and Viktoriya didn't think the odds favored the captain. But, when did they ever?

Vasin had ordered her to send out patrols. Keep an eye on

enemy movement, and ascertain where they might try and cross. Finishing her tea Viktoriya said, "Let's roll."

"Yest, ma'am," said Rozhkov. "Mount up people. Time to earn your pay." As he ushered everyone into the waiting heavily armed Bumerang infantry fighting vehicle.

Its tires had been fitted with snow tracks, connecting the eight wheels into pairs, turning the IFV into a tracked vehicle. It worked, it wasn't perfect, but good enough for today's patrol.

The plan was a quick sneak and peek at the enemy positions.

If everything proceeded as planned they would be in and out before anyone knew of their presence.

Viktoriya took her place in the back sat opposite to Rozhkov. They moved off suddenly, and her stomach lurched as vehicle slid sideways.

Time passed as they made their way through the snow. The vehicle descended a slope then bounced up as it climbed over something before straightening up and continuing on.

Rozhkov sat monitoring their progress, spoke, "Ma'am, we've got enemy activity ahead."

Sooka. Had they been spotted? She pulled up the IFVs feeds that detected small arms fire. Viktoriya overlaid the satellite feed of the area.

The firing emanated from the enemy's forward line. The one they'd come out today to observe. But, the shots were not in response to the IFV, which was still behind a low hill.

There was literally no point in the enemy firing at them, even if they had detected the IFVs movement. Or, at least no point firing small arms when they could call in artillery.

"Ma'am, your orders?"

Viktoriya took a moment to weigh up the options. "Get ready to debus, Rozhkov."

She clambered up and opened the top hatch. The freezing cold air whipped past her as the IFV stormed up the hill. As they crested the ridge, she could see two people running for cover.

Too small for the satellite feeds to pick up.

Viktoriya shouted down, "Put us on a course to intercept them."

1. COMMAND POST

Seventh Rota Head Quarters, Tver
180 Kilometers North West of Moskva
Kapitán Grigory Lenkov

Grigory stood in his power armor with the helmet off. He stared into the darkness, wanting to step out of the stuffy air of the tent.

Part of him desired to once again lead troops into battle.

He longed for any excuse to give him the opportunity to join in the oncoming action. However, he accepted that his role was no longer to be a shooter in the line of battle, but to command.

"Excuse me, Kapitán Lenkov," said Gruzdev, seventh company's master sergeant. "It's time, sir."

"It always is, Starshiná Gruzdev."

Grigory turned his back on the night and entered the tent. He ignored the stench of sweat and went to study the tactical table.

He ached from the tension of doing nothing but watching and waiting. He would've preferred to be back in charge of third platoon, but they now had a new lieutenant to replace him after his promotion.

Rapid promotion to replace casualties having become routine

after decades of officers rising slowly through the ranks in peacetime.

Grigory chaffed at being a lieutenant for eight years before the war, waiting for dead-men's shoes to move up.

Ironically, it was precisely the fact that more men were dying that he'd been promoted to captain.

Real-time updates from seventh company's platoons were being automatically fed into computer. The data created an ever-evolving map of the front the company covered.

Unfortunately, the map systems were unable to access the satellite feeds, which meant that parts of map were static, based on last known observations.

Until new satellites could be launched, it was like being back in the twentieth century when commanders used paper maps and markers for units.

Grigory was therefore grateful for what he had, because using physical maps and having staff manually updating the position of his units would put him further behind what was actually happening on the line.

What he saw in front of him happening in real time.

Should he wish, he could call up computer-generated virtual images for closer study. Running and re-running events. And or choosing to look at the same scene from more than one viewpoint.

Grigory scratched at an itch.

The only problem with this facility was losing track of the changes in the *battlespace*, which occurred faster than the time it took to watch and analyze events as they happened.

That had cost the previous commander of seventh company, and those with him, their lives.

Grigory wasn't going to let that happen now.

Instead, he relied on the command posts artificial intelligence systems. Using the expert systems, created from heuristic algorithms or human experience, to make the best decisions he could.

The trouble was it demanded his complete attention. And it was impossible to know the outcome of an engagement, until too late.

Tonight, his former senior sergeant led first squad on a reconnaissance mission. A mission to discover what the enemy was doing in an area on part of the map that was no longer under satellite observation.

The feed from Rozhkov's squad went black after they debussed from their IFV. Although this was expected, it now meant the map would not be updated from first squad's feeds until they transmitted what they'd found.

Another problem of constant feeds was that the transmissions were point sources that could be tracked.

In the bigger battlespace this wasn't generally a problem as tracking the feeds in real time was impractical. But a lone squad moving around was easy to track.

Grigory wished he could've convinced Colonel Korolev of the benefit of staging a diversion. However, the colonel had informed him that signal analysis suggested that the enemy were not preparing an operation.

All of the enemy's communications suggested they were still consolidating their recent gains.

Korolev was undoubtedly reporting the truth.

But Grigory's gut told him the enemy were creating a smokescreen to hide their true intentions. With winter coming they would be planning an attack. P prevent Russian forces digging in.

Or at least that was what he'd be doing if the positions were reversed.

Major Borodin had then proceeded to remind him of his area

of responsibility and to leave INTEL matters to others with more experience in such matters.

Borodin claimed he had years of experience under his belt, but it seemed more like a lot of the food and drink to Grigory.

Now he waited.

Hoping that tonight's reconnaissance mission was routine. But, the war had long since made the "routine" the unexpected outcome of any day.

Then a blip appeared.

The icon on the map colored it red, an enemy unit began moving towards their lines. Grigory's gut tightened. It was the enemy unit that Rozhkov had been sent to observe.

Something must have happened, rousing the enemy into action.

"Gruzdev, sound the alert," Grigory said, and then listening to his master sergeant as he started issuing orders to the other platoons.

He called up battalion HQ and gave a brief report; enemy contact moving toward their lines.

Without satellite coverage he must rely on feeds from his company net. So far, the only unit in contact with the enemy was off the net.

Minutes later that changed.

Grigory monitored Lieutenant Morozova call in artillery barrage as her third platoon made contact with the enemy.

His map updated the information.

Blue icons change from standby to alert status. The feed showed the bearing and speed of the enemy as it breached the perimeter of their forward line.

The image on the table's map screen glitched.

A moment where everything went fuzzy, then the image updated. The enemy were using electronic counter-counter measures against them.

Grigory felt a sense of unease.

The interference increased.

From what he could see, and the reports from Morozova, the artillery barrage failed to stop the enemy attack.

The tank, he couldn't believe it was just one tank, had advanced so fast that it had moved past the pre-registered kill-box. First and second platoons moved to intercept the intruder.

Each platoon consisted of three T90AM-U tanks.

The map updated their position as they moved into contact. One-by-one the six tank icons turned from green to red.

A dreadful apprehension spurred Grigory to action. "Gruzdev, we need to evacuate the command post now!"

"What, sir?"

Grigory called up battalion HQ and reported that the enemy were heading towards his command post. "Grab what you can, we're about to be overrun."

"Yest, Kapitán!" said Starshiná Gruzdev. "Serzhánt Volkova get the truck started."

Grigory waited, his stomach churning, monitoring the enemy tank's progress as the people around him packed what they could.

He could smell his own fear as he heard an explosion in the distance, followed by the sound of a rotary cannon.

"We go now, people!" Grigory shouted, gesturing everyone out.

Outside, Volkova's truck pulled up and he jumped into the cab with her.

Gruzdev and junior sergeant Anosov were boarding the other vehicle that made up seventh company's headquarters transport element.

The trucks engines roared in unison as they both accelerated away from the command post. In the distance, a massive tank could be seen, bearing down on their position faster than it had any right to do.

Grigory tried to lock his suit into the truck's seat restraining system as it bounced over the ground. Volkova having been spurred by the sight of the enemy tank floored the accelerator.

Faster is good.

Whether they would be fast enough would be another matter. They might be able to outrace the tank, but not its gun's shells.

He heard the boom of the tank firing behind them.

2. ATTACK

Seventh Rota Head Quarters, Tver
180 Kilometers North West of Moskva
Serzhánt Alisa Volkova

Alisa heard the boom from the enemy tank. The glare from explosion lit up the night, illuminating the two escaping trucks.

Beside her Lenkov was trying to strap himself into his seat as the truck bounced violently up and down.

Alisa had been shocked when Lenkov ordered the command post evacuated.

She didn't believe an enemy tank could move so quickly. But her disbelief didn't slow its advance one iota. Alisa knew the tank meant death, and she didn't want to die.

She muttered a prayer.

Promised God she would be a good girl from now on. She would even go to church. She promised.

Alisa pressed the accelerator to the floor.

The engine revved, and the wheels spun, churning up mud, before the traction control took over.

Another boom and flash followed.

The other truck was hit.

It flew up into the air and flipped over. The shock of the blast shook them as parts rained down.

Then another boom rang out as the other truck exploded.

Gruzdev and Anosov must have been killed instantly. Alisa hoped for their sake they didn't suffer.

She gripped the steering wheel so hard that her hands hurt.

Another explosion went off next to them. Her truck rose up and went spinning through the air before crashing onto its side. Lenkov flailed around like a broken puppet.

The force of the impact knocked her senseless.

Alisa came around to the sound of squealing tracks approaching.

Time seemed to slow. Frozen by fear, she didn't dare to move in case the tank noticed her. Alisa felt the cab of the truck shake as the enemy tank drove by.

"Thank you, God," Alisa said, over and over again, rocking in her restraining harness.

She realized Lenkov was not saying anything. Alisa looked down on her right and saw where he had been thrown when the truck overturned.

He'd taken a beating from the brunt of the explosion.

She grabbed a handle and released her straps, letting her body turn and slide down, and then let go to drop beside him. Alisa checked his ABE-OBR:6U, Activniy Bronirovanniy Ekzoskelet medical readout.

Condensation covered the inside of his power armor's visor.

His medical monitor listed broken ribs, a hairline fracture of the skull, a broken left arm, internal contusions, blunt force trauma—and breathing.

Alisa noticed a medical alert flashing in her HUD. *Pasna, danger.* Overpressure limit of suit exceeded.

Spasibo, so much for stating the obvious.

The captain was unconscious. But, one thing was certain, she couldn't wait here for him to come around. Time was not on their side.

The enemy had attacked, and as sure as eggs-were-eggs, there would be more enemy coming through here soon.

The question was how to get out of the over turned truck?

Simple was best. Not always the easiest way, but keeping things simple usually was the best course.

Alisa started kicking the roof of the truck to make a hole. She used her power armor suit to rip the roof back. She bent over, crouched down, and crawled her way out.

Standing up, she peeled the roof off the cab, grateful the truck was an unarmored soft-skin vehicle. Then she dragged Lenkov out.

However, Alisa knew she wouldn't get far carrying him. If she tried, it was likely they would be caught, and that would be that. No guarantees what would happen next.

She needed to find somewhere close by to hole up.

The other truck was still burning, illuminating the ground around seventh company's former command post. Then she remembered there was a hut a few hundred meters away.

Used by local hunters.

Alisa had spotted it when they'd originally set up the command post's perimeter scanners. It wasn't much, but it was tucked away and hidden from casual observation.

Alisa lifted Lenkov up over her shoulder.

She considered taking him out of his power armor because its systems were offline. But, that would mean two trips. And less trips seemed to her to be the better strategy when the clock was ticking.

She followed the tracks of the enemy tank as far as she could.

Then Alisa turned off and headed towards her goal.

It began to snow, so she hurried to the hut. It was rudimentary, but it had a roof and a door. She could use foliage as camouflage to hide it from sight.

Alisa dragged Lenkov inside and laid him down. She checked his suit's medical monitor. He still lived, and at least now she'd gotten him to shelter.

It was the best she could do.

She was under no illusion about the harshness of winter. The hut would serve as a temporary base, but they'd need food and water.

Alisa went back to the truck. Thirty minutes had gone by since the attack.

She was wary and had her rifle ready. What if the enemy came back now? She must work fast.

Her truck had been knocked over by the blast, leaving it fit for nothing but the scrapyard. It hadn't taken a direct hit from the enemy tank, so its cargo had survived, strewn all around.

Alisa slung her rifle and began to work.

The truck had been loaded up with everything seventh company's command post needed to function. Alisa knew that there were supplies here essential for her survival.

She started sifting through the boxes scattered by the force of the blast.

Even with her power armor on she sweated.

Her suit did its best to compensate, but moisture dripped down her face.

She lifted her visor, and wish she hadn't. Freezing air whipped across her face. It stung, leaving her nose numb from the cold.

She found a jerry can of water, not yet frozen, and another of fuel. In the cab was her backpack. Loaded up, Alisa went back to the hut.

Snowflakes whirled around her. Snow had begun to buildup on the ground.

Back at the hut, Lenkov lay where she'd left him, still

unconscious. His suit readings now showed him running a fever and his temperature was high.

His suit administered medication.

Alisa knew she would need to retrieve the truck's medical kit. But, even that wouldn't guarantee his survival.

Alisa trudged back to the site, cursing the snowfall for making it harder to walk and thanking it, since it would help hide her tracks.

This time she began by pulling off the tarpaulin off the rear of the truck. Using it and a couple of branches tided together at one end, she made a travois.

Onto it she put boxes of rations, the medical kit, and a portable generator to recharge the suits. There was also a space heater, so she grabbed that too.

Alisa lashed the tarpaulin with some rope to stop her load from coming loose, and started dragging it. Without the suit, she could not have pulled the load at all.

With her suit, she could just about do it.

The challenge came when she left the path made by the tank's tracks. She slid and fell several times on the increasingly slippery ground.

Back at the hut she unpacked and stash the gear. Then checked Lenkov, before making her way back to the truck with the tarpaulin.

She found the captain's pack, some more tools, and put them on the tarpaulin. Alisa dragged it behind her to obscure her tracks in the snow.

When she got back to the hut, she felt pleased at covering her trail.

Alisa checked on Lenkov again. He was hanging in. So she dropped his pack beside him.

Alisa went back outside the hut. She staked two corners of the tarpaulin into the ground and then pulled the opposite edge up to make a windbreak in front of the door.

Getting snowed in would just be a bit of a sooka.

The tarpaulin also camouflaged the entrance to the hut. Alisa went inside and shut the door. Out in the darkness, she thought she heard the sound of armor coming, but it might be her imagination.

The chances of not being discovered seemed slim, but what else could she do?

Leaving Lenkov behind would likely be leaving him to die. She couldn't in good conscience do that.

But she was under no illusion about the chances of her living. As for making it back to friendly lines, they seemed slim to none.

She shivered despite the warmth of her suit.

Putting those thoughts away, Alisa decided it was time to heat the place up.

Then she could get Lenkov and herself out of their suits, and do what she could with the first aid kit she'd retrieved.

It was going to be a long night.

3. WOLF

Tver, 180 Kilometers North West of Moskva
Kapitán Grigory Lenkov

Grigory heard a noise and struggled to open his eyes. Every part of him hurt. He couldn't move, and for a moment feared he was paralyzed.

Instead, he found himself in his sleeping bag, lying on a bunkbed.

"Good to see you back in the land of the living, Kapitán," said a woman's voice.

He tried to recall who she was.

Where was he? It looked like a room. Yes, it was a room, but then everything went blurry, and he struggled to bring his surroundings back into focus.

He remembered who the voice belonged to. "Is that you, Volkova?"

"Tak tochno, sir. It's good to see you awake. I wasn't sure you would make it."

Grigory remembered the truck racing away from a tank. Not just any enemy tank, but a monstrous machine.

He sat up, wincing at every movement, as he wriggled his arms free. One arm was black and blue. The other had a cast on it.

He felt light-headed.

"Here's something to drink," said Volkova handing him a cup of soup. "I'll heat up something solid for you."

"What's happening?"

Clearly he hadn't died, but how did he get to be staring at the walls of a wooden hut? Whatever this place was, it clearly wasn't a first aid station.

Volkova sat, squatted down on the floor. She was fiddling with a ration pack over a small field stove. Grigory's carbine and backpack were to one side.

At the other end of the room both suits of power armor were stood by what must be the door to the hut.

He was confused. None of this made any sense. Just sitting up caused him excruciating pain.

"Here, take this," said Volkova, which startled him.

What just happened. The sergeant had put a tablet in his hand.

"Swallow it, drink some more soup, and eat this food."

He did as he was told. After eating he felt oddly tired and fell asleep again.

Next time he woke Grigory still hurt all over, but his head was clearer. "What time is it?"

Volkova was asleep in her sleeping bag on a bunk opposite, didn't answer him. The inside of the hut wasn't hot, but neither was it freezing. He got out of his bag and sat on the edge of the bed.

He saw Volkova looking at him.

"Good to see you up, sir."

"What time is it?" Grigory had to know how long it had been since the attack.

He couldn't remember why it might be important, but it was. He was having difficulty in concentrating. A wave of anxiety swept over him. He felt frightened, like something bad was going to happen.

Grigory stood up and began to sway.

"I think you should sit down, before you fall, sir."

The impertinence of addressing a superior officer in such a manner made him angry.

Then he felt dizzy, and the room became blurry. Grigory decided to sit on the floor. He flopped down gracelessly.

That was strange.

He felt like he'd just run a marathon.

Grigory lost track of time and found Volkova had gotten up and was helping him back into his sleeping bag. He must have a concussion.

Hours passed. Grigory would fall asleep, then wake in pain. Then fall asleep again.

In his dreams a giant tank laughed at him. Calling him stupid. There were dancing bears too.

Grigory wasn't sure why there were bears doing Cossack dances. It all made a strange kind of sense, until he woke up to find he'd been dreaming.

Now Volkova was making another meal. He'd lost track of time again.

"Some porridge, sir," she said, passing him a cup with a spoon.

He felt ravenous and wolfed it down.

"Spasibo."

"You're welcome, sir. It's good to see you eat. It means I can stop worrying about how badly you were concussed."

Grigory realized that he was lucky to be alive, and it was all down to this woman saving him.

"How bad is it?"

"Gruzdev and Anosov are both dead. We're stuck behind enemy lines. It's been snowing."

Grigory let that sink in, mulling the implications. He asked, "How long?"

"It's been three days since the attack. The good news is that the enemy didn't find us when they went past," said Volkova, who added, "and as you can see I salvaged some supplies. We have fuel, water, and food."

"So I see."

"What are your orders, sir?"

A good question, and one that he thought Volkova had asked out of respect, rather than any real need for him to tell her what had to be done.

"We need to make a move. Any suggestions Serzhánt Volkova?"

He hoped she would take the initiative, as he wasn't sure he was capable of doing so. She had kept him alive, and under the circumstances the odds were not in their favor that this was a permanent proposition.

Then again, they lived in an imperfect world.

"I suggest we move as soon as you're able. I've made a sled, which we can use to pull our supplies. It will increase our chances of making it back to our own lines, sir."

Grigory paused to consider the options. His mind was fugged. Not wanting to seem as if he was deliberately stretching out his decision, he answered, "Let me know how I can help."

"Spasibo, sir. But I have it covered. If you could rest and recuperate that would be a big help."

How diplomatic of her.

Grigory nodded, and before he knew it, he had fallen into a deep sleep.

His dreams were still weird as shit.

The bears were now singing, "Katyusha," in a rising crescendo that never ended.

4. PREPARATIONS

Tver, 180 Kilometers North West of Moskva
Serzhánt Alisa Volkova

Another dawn. Alisa worked outside the hut, as a cold wind whistled past her. Wielding the sharpened edge of her Spetsnaz shovel as an axe to hack through a sapling.

She felt all alone, lost in a sea of white as she struggled to move.

Even with her suit's ski-shoes she found it hard to do any work or walk.

Finally, she finished sawing through the trunk, and let it drop to the ground. Alisa could taste the saltiness of her sweat. The task left her feeling exhausted, but she still had a lot more to do.

Alisa walked alongside the tree, using it to stop herself from toppling into the snow. She took her improvised axe and started lopping off the branches.

Every thunk of the shovel against the wood meant progress.

Progress seemed slow and Alisa struggled, feeling the strain as she neared finishing the task of chopping. Without the help of her power armor, she doubted she could've finished the job.

Even so, it had taken all of her strength and pushed her to the limits of her endurance.

Feeling her heart racing, Alisa took a deep breath. She paused for a moment or two to get her strength back for the next part of her project.

Satisfied with what she'd done, Alisa started on the harder task of splitting the sapling into two, to make the runners for a sled.

If only Lenkov were able to help. But he lay asleep inside the hut, recovering from his injuries.

Alisa had seen the bruises on his body when she took him out of his suit.

The man's body was covered in ugly red, black splotches. She had a few of her own, but nothing like the amount covering his body.

She was surprised he lived.

Explosive concussion killed. Most civilians didn't understand that the blast from an explosion could kill.

Luckily, for both her and Lenkov, their suits had protected them from the overpressure. Nothing had penetrated their armor.

But Lenkov had been unstrapped when the truck tumbled. As, a result, he'd received blunt force trauma, from being thrown around the cab.

His suit couldn't protect him from that.

Alisa suspected he may have further injuries from being crushed inside his suit. But, he was still alive. Being alive being better than being dead, even in war.

Pleased with her work she went back into the hut to drag out one of the bunk beds, which she planned to use as a body for her sled.

Lenkov still slept.

For a moment, she thought he had stopped breathing. Then he coughed, turned, and continued to sleep.

Feeling thirsty, she drank some water. Gulping it down she almost choked. Recovering her composure, she dragged the bunkbed frame outside.

Alisa had plenty of army cord, and began by placing the first runner to the bottom of a bed-frame, tying them together.

She feel into a rhythm of, wrap, twist, and then knot. She repeated the process on the other side.

When finished, she had a sled with a rope attached in a loop for them to pull it with.

She was pleased, and hoped that her handiwork would stand up for the journey ahead. Her father wouldn't say it was pretty, but he would be proud of her all the same.

Alisa was grateful for all her batyanya taught her before he died.

She still missed him, and probably always would. His death had left a hole in her and her mother's lives.

For a moment she felt maudlin, but then she heard a rumble of thunder in the distance. The thunder of artillery. The fighting was still going on.

Because their side was in retreat, every day that they delayed meant two days' more walking. That would increase the chances of them being spotted as they made their way back to their own lines.

She pushed those thoughts out of her head.

This was not a time for doubts. Alisa couldn't let her fear of what might happen get in the way of what she needed to do.

She needed to focus on her goal, take it one step at a time.

Her problem was surviving the journey she was about to undertake with Lenkov. The captain might not be able to cope with the pain that the walking would cause him.

If she had to, she would put him on the sled and drag him to safety.

She would do whatever it took to get them back to their lines, or die trying.

5. MARCH OR DIE

Tver, 180 Kilometers North West of Moskva
Kapitán Grigory Lenkov

Grigory woke to the sound of Volkova's power armor moving near him. She had her visor up and said something.

For a moment, he puzzled over what, before realizing it must be time to leave.

Struggling out of his sleeping bag he stood up.

Grigory reached out to the bunkbed for support as the pain hit him. He hurt so much he thought he would scream.

He stifled a cry as the pain threatened to overwhelm him.

Then he smelt something stale. It was him. Three days of sweating without a wash and he stank.

"I've made you something to eat, and tea, sir."

"I need to wash."

"Yes, you do, sir," said Volkova who pointed at a bowl on the floor, next to a plate and a cup. "You can eat and get cleaned up. I'll pack your gear. I've put out clean underwear for you too. Promise I won't look."

Grigory started to snap back at her, but stopped. He realized

Volkova had made a joke to hide the dire circumstances they were in. Or how bad he looked.

He stripped and used a flannel to clean his face, and armpits, and finally his private parts. Freezing cold air swept over him as Volkova went out of the hut taking the last of their supplies.

He got dressed, rolled his soiled clothes up, and put them in a ziplock bag before stuffing them in his pack.

As he finished eating Volkova came back in.

"It's time, sir. You might want to take a painkiller."

Grigory took the offered tablet, and washed it down with the last of the tea. Although the food had been bland but filling, the tea was sweet and delicious.

He felt stronger for drinking it.

It was time to find out what he was made of. This woman had done everything for him. Now, he must show that he was worth the time and effort she'd spent keeping him alive.

He owed it to Russia. He owed it to himself. Most of all, he owed it to her.

Volkova helped him don his basic armor and then guided him into the exoskeleton frame. She adjusted the fittings, and Grigory did his best not to wince.

Once in the suit, it took a lot of the weight off him. He slung his carbine, knowing that if the time came to use it, he would probably die.

Still, the effort he'd taken to get ready had warmed him up.

The exoskeleton's medical scanner initiated the wounded trooper protocol. The suit would do most of the work to keep him upright and moving.

But choosing to do so would use more power.

That would reduce their chances of making it back. All he had to do was bear the pain of walking. He could do that. Rather than taking energy from the suite, he overrode the protocol and took a step.

The suit didn't fall over, a victory for him. A small victory, but a much needed one, if he were to face the trek which lay ahead of them both.

Volkova opened the door and led him out into the whiteness.

His first step sank into the snow.

He lifted his other leg and his suit deployed the ski-shoes in response. Grigory felt resistance as the suit enabled him to stand on top of the snow.

Volkova asked, "Ready, sir?" Offering him a rope to pull.

He stared across the bleak winter landscape.

The trunks of trees sticking up out of the whiteness. A frozen waste they needed to cross to survive. One that would kill them if they didn't take care where they stepped.

He remembered he'd been asked a question. "Which way?"

"Southeast. I've got a route planned and set into our suits navigation system. We got lucky with having the coordinates for where we were, sir."

That was one way of looking at their situation. Her unbridled optimism in the face of adversity amazed him.

"Are you sure you're truly Russian, Volkova?"

She laughed. "We've run out of vodka, Kapitán. Remember, you ordered me to share it with the rest of the platoon."

He laughed. That seemed like a lifetime ago.

"No vodka?"

Volkova smiled. "Perhaps a small flask may be hidden about my person."

He smiled back. Good to know that even under these circumstances that his supply sergeant still had the wherewithal to have a small supply of vodka on her.

It showed that at least one thing remained right with the world.

All journeys begin with a single step. Grigory grimaced as he took a step. Then he followed it with another, and then another.

He wanted to laugh, but didn't have the strength. He wanted to cry, but was afraid if he did so he would never be able to stop.

Then he would die. His options were march or die.

Dying was overrated. March it was. And so they began.

He started humming to himself.

It helped with the pain.

6. A WALK IN THE SNOW

Somewhere East of Tver
Serzhánt Alisa Volkova

Alisa's HUD display kept track of their time and progress. She and Lenkov were halfway through the third day of their journey. So far, managing to make good progress.

The sound of their march fell into a rhythm as their feet crunched through the snow.

Sweating from the effort of pulling the sled. But Lenkov had a much worse time of it. So far, they'd managed to cover nearly forty kilometers.

If they could keep this pace up, they would cover another five kilometers by the end of the day. Alisa could taste the nearness of the end of their journey. Safety lay ahead.

But tomorrow she'd have to be alert to the possibility of their enemy spotting them as they tried to pass through the lines.

She felt rather than heard Lenkov fall.

Alisa stopped walking. It almost took more effort than carrying on walking mindlessly. She looked back.

Lenkov lay on the ground a couple of steps behind her.

His power armor adaptive camouflage turned the suit a dirty-white. It was difficult to tell where the man ended and the snow began. Green splotches of webbing were all she could actually make out.

She dropped the rope and clambered over to him.

"Sir, are you OK?"

Lenkov didn't reply, his suit's medical monitor indicated he was unconscious. That couldn't be good. But he wasn't dead, at least not yet.

She plugged a cable from her suit to slave Lenkov's suit to hers. Alisa pulled up a sub-routine to allow her to get him to stand. She then led him to the sled.

Alisa left Lenkov by the side as she rearranged their supplies. What little they had left.

With only enough fuel for one more day. Water for another, and tonight they would run out of everything apart from a couple of slabs of butter. And her small flask of vodka that she'd saved for the final push.

When she'd planned the journey, she'd made her best guess on how long it would take them to get back to their lines. Up to now everything had gone according to plan. Up to now.

She kicked herself for not retrieving more. But, in her heart, she knew they'd struggled to pull what they started with. If anything, the lightning of the load, helped them travel further each day. One of those things which was counter-intuitive.

Carry more to survive longer, but carry too much and you can't get far at all. It was a conundrum that all armies faced. The pair of them didn't constitute an army, but that didn't make the problem go away.

Alisa turned the captain around and made his suit sit on the sled. Then she tied a rope around Lenkov to prevent him from falling off. Satisfied that he was secure, she went back and picked up the rope and took a step.

She sunk into the snow, not moving. The sled stuck.

With the captain on top the sled became too heavy for her to pull. Alisa took a deep breath and gritted her teeth, straining with all her strength. Her feet dug deeper into the snow. It moved around her, forming a depression, but she continued pulling on the rope.

Her suit whined in protest.

"Sooka!" Alisa screamed as she felt the sled move, then stop. "Da-Vhy sooka."

Urging herself to move her sorry ass, she heaved again, leaning all her weight onto the rope. The sled followed, the pressure easing as she gained momentum. One step, then another.

Then she felt firmer snow underfoot. The sled began to slide more easily.

Alisa kept going not daring to pause to catch her breath. To stop moving would be the end of them. Giving up now was not an option.

She must march.

Alisa knew from the start she might have to pull the captain. She had to believe that every step she took, took her one step closer to safety.

A red line on her HUD marked out the route.

Leading them across the winter whiteness.

Just keep marching, one step at a time.

7. LENKOV

Somewhere East of Tver
Kapitán Grigory Lenkov

Grigory woke to find himself lying on the sled with Volkova pulling it through the snow.

His put aside the discomfort of finding himself humiliated by his weakness, and tried to move his aching limbs. His body had stiffened up so much that he could hardly move.

And his mouth was dry.

He found his suit's water feed. He took a long suck, and then another. The water was warm, and it didn't make the pain any less. But the relief from having a drink was profound.

Grigory clenched his teeth as he forced himself to move.

Then he cursed, finally managing to sit upright. How Volkova managed to keep going was beyond him. All he knew was that he owed his life to her.

His movement caught Volkova's attention.

She stopped and turned to face him. No doubt taking this moment of distraction to catch her breath.

She shouted across to him, "Good, there looks to be a place

where we can shelter tonight, and I could do with a bit of help, sir."

Grigory looked around at the winter landscape.

He came from the city, and the countryside that all looked the same to him. He vaguely remembered that Volkova's family hailed from a small village outside of Arkhangelsk.

She came over and helped him off the sled.

"I can plug you into my suit if you wish, sir?"

He took Grigory a moment to understand what she meant. "No, I can manage. I'll fall over if I can't."

"Yest, Kapitán. As you wish."

Was she mocking him? He couldn't tell.

He must have fallen before. How else could he have ended up on the sled? But he could find no memory of what had happened.

Volkova indicated he should help her pull the sled across the undulating plain of whiteness that he found so disorientating. They made their way towards what he now recognized as some bushes.

Or at least the tops of some bushes.

The ground fell away in a gentle slope before rising again in the distance. The wind blew across the snow, lifting it up and creating small flurries that made it hard to tell what he was looking at.

"I'm going to start digging, sir. Whatever you can unload will be a big help."

Volkova was like one of those heroes you hear about in byliny —*folksongs*, an example "to be," inspired by stories from something "that was."

He unloaded the sled, sorting out those things he knew they'd need for tonight. Setting up the generator to recharge their suits and the heater to keep them warm.

Grigory lifted the fuel can, which felt disturbingly light.

He paused, sodden by sweat from the exertion, grateful that

his suit would prevent him from freezing after sweating so much. The suit's exoskeleton musculature whined as he turned to ask Volkova what she wanted done next.

He still marveled at Volkova's ability to produce different shelters according to the lay of the land. Yesterday she'd piled snow on top of all their gear and then dug through and created a snow shelter.

Tonight, she had dug a hole.

What he thought was a bush turned out to be a tree. Not a very big tree, but a tree all the same. Volkova dug down to make a hole under the branches.

A narrow trench led inside where a raised area of snow had been left.

Obviously, he must have been staring because Volkova stopped to speak.

"Practice. and my silovaya bronya. Without my suit I couldn't have managed."

"You read my mind, Serzhánt."

"It's amazing what one can do when faced with being frozen to death. Just got to make a firewall to reflect the heat and act as a windbreak, then we can eat."

Eating sounded good, but Grigory noticed that they were down to the last of their rations, some sausages and pickled vegetables.

When they finished eating, all they'd have left were a couple of packs of frozen butter.

So, rather than wolf the food down tonight, he took the time to savor each mouthful.

It could well be the last meal he'd eat.

8. DAY FOUR

Ten kilometers West of Dobna
Serzhánt Alisa Volkova

She knew that this was their last day. Alisa might not die today, but their chances of survival after today were slim to none.

Now all of their fuel had been used up.

Without fuel for the generator they couldn't recharge their power armor suits. Or the heater which they used to melt water.

Though, with wood she knew she could start a fire to melt water for drinking.

But a fire would increase the chances of the enemy spotting them. And she couldn't stop the inevitable moment when the suits would stop working.

Staying alive in the cold without their suits would be impossible.

Last night the temperature had fallen to minus six degrees centigrade. And she'd been grateful for the shelter's protection.

Alisa looked over their supplies.

They no longer needed the sled. It would only slow them down. The time had come to abandon it.

She decided to take the tarpaulin and army cord, her shovel, and all their remaining water, putting it in her pack.

No point in burdening Lenkov, given his propensity to fall unconscious.

To prevent that, they would have to plug their suits together. Slave his suit to hers. The cost would be restricting her freedom of movement.

Alisa checked her suit's comms.

The satellites were up, and she'd managed to get their location, and confirm their track's bearing. By her reckoning, it was less than two kilometers to the rear of the enemy lines.

Once through them, they'd face another eight kilometers of walking to get to the forward edge of friendly lines.

Alisa weighed up making a call, but the transmission would give them away. Not their exact location, perhaps, but that a Russian unit was behind Visegrád Baltic Alliance lines.

On balance, it would be safer to wait and call after passing through the enemy lines. Of course, getting this far didn't mean they would make it through.

One way or another today was kgnech naya, *the end* of their journey.

Lenkov was awake, so she gave him one of the slabs of butter, which was all that remained to eat. Alisa pulled out her small knife and sliced a piece off the slab.

The butter was hard as cheese.

"Not bad," Alisa said. It wasn't what she would have considered offering as a zakuska, *a snack* to be eaten when drinking vodka, but it would do.

Pulling out her flask she made a toast, "Bóo-deem zda-ró-vye." *To our health*, before taking a swig of vodka.

Lenkov took the flask she offered. "Nostrovia. K-zhizni."

To life indeed, Alisa thought. If she were still alive at the end of this day, she would go to church and pray to give thanks. But God helps those who help themselves.

Alisa finished eating the butter, shared the last of their vodka, and stood to get back into her power armor.

She helped Lenkov suit up as he was still stiff and unable to fasten his suit by himself.

"My trigger finger still works," said Lenkov.

If it came down to relying on either of them shooting, she doubted they would make it to the end of the day alive.

Still, if she must die today she would take an enemy with her. But Rozhkov would be mad at her for dying, and miss her too.

Alisa held onto that thought. It would keep her from making mistakes.

Caution and patience were their best allies for surviving the day. Caution, patience, and all the endurance they could muster.

Alisa checked that she'd put everything they needed in her backpack, remembering to take the emergency fire-starter kit too. They both carried their weapons and ammo, some flares, and three grenades each.

Pretty much the lightest load she'd ever taken into the field.

But what Alisa carried might help keep them alive one more night.

Whether being alive for one more day, in the middle of a Russian winter without their power armor suits was desirable, was another matter. But where there's life, there's hope.

And Alisa was determined to hang onto her life for as long as she could.

Ready, Alisa scrambled up out of their hole in the ground, and felt the full force of the wind blowing from the east. The direction that they needed to walk.

Her suit's heating element compensated for the cold, but mindful of the power drain, she lowered the automatic thermostat setting.

No need to heat the suit when the walk would keep her warm enough.

Lenkov struggled in the snow, so she offered him a hand to help him up.

He was clearly stiff and in a great deal of pain. But the captain had guts and determination. He got up and let go.

They started walking. Their suits were like ghosts against the snow.

With luck, they wouldn't be spotted. With luck.

If only they'd been luckier escaping the tank. Yes, she and the captain had been lucky not to have been killed when the tank fired at their truck.

But in Alisa's experience, you made luck through hard work and determination.

Hours passed as they marched through the snow.

9. LIMITS

West of Dobna
Kapitán Grigory Lenkov

Grigory ski-shoes slid across the snow. After hours of struggling he'd gotten into the rhythm of push and slide, the suit's gyros keeping him upright.

They'd worked their way up a slight rise and now he followed Volkova down the other-side of the slope, and into a gully of a frozen river.

He was sweating from the exertion of the march.

It meant that his suit no longer needed to keep him warm. Instead, it dehumidified the air circulating around his body. Getting too hot and sweaty could lead to dehydration or hypothermia.

Russian power armor might not be the most advanced in the world. However, the suits were optimized for Russian winters.

But so were the ones the Visegrád Baltic Alliance gave to their troops.

Grigory crouched to keep his head below the ridge. He

desperately wanted to stop and rest, but rest wasn't an option. He could rest when dead.

They made their way along the treacherous ice, using the gully to hide their movements from prying eyes. The enemy were spread out to defend a line against a counter-attack by the Ground Forces.

A line he and Volkova had to pass through without being detected.

They'd spotted a sentry ahead. Fortunately, facing the other way.

Grigory couldn't blame the soldier for this failing. They were, after all, not supposed to be here.

Two people, all alone, out in the middle of a Russian winter was the very definition of unlikely. Even sniper teams acted as part of a larger force, with support.

And he and Volkova were no sniper team. Just two soldiers trapped behind enemy lines.

Volkova used an electronic periscope to scan out the route.

While waiting, realizing how thirsty he felt, he took another sip of water, and then sucked down some more. He shivered. Having stopped walking his body cooled down.

Despite being sheltered from the wind, the freezing cold chilled his suit.

Volkova asked, "You ready?"

Was he ready? Grigory nodded, yes. He was as ready as he would ever be.

"We're going to go right, keeping the ridgeline on our left. We might have to crawl some of the way."

Tethered together, Grigory's power armor could take images from her feed. He saw what she saw. A shallow fold in the ground ahead which they would use to get around the guard.

But there was "no might" about the crawling.

"I'm good." Because what else could he say?

He could think of lots of things to say, but none of them relevant, appropriate, or helpful.

Volkova stared at him. The woman assessed him and then unplugged the tether to his suit and said, "Let's go."

Volkova, heaved herself over the top of the gully and began crawling past the guard's position. A flurry of loose snow descended the bank as Grigory followed.

His limbs felt like leaden weights, his muscles burned with the effort of getting up the side of the bank. The pain of pulling himself along was agonizing.

He flopped onto the snow.

Unable to move any further. Ahead of him Volkova crawled behind some cover. If she could do it, so could he.

Grigory crawled forward, pushing his legs into the snow, and using his elbows to gain traction. Now he began to get too hot again.

He felt like a furnace burning, but it kept the coldness of the winter at bay.

He stopped to take another sip of water. Then moved forward again. He followed in the trail plowed by Volkova's passage.

If there was anyone looking from above, they would be easy to spot.

Shots rang out around him. They'd been spotted. Volkova started shooting at something behind him.

Adrenaline course through him and Grigory raced towards safety.

He slid down next to her.

"Drone!"

Grigory turned to look, trying to locate what Volkova shot at. Then he saw a movement. A white spot against the sky.

She hit it and then shot another.

Not one drone, but a swarm of drones. Drones could be deadly, swarms especially so. But, drones were small and fragile.

Volkova made short work of the swarm.

Then Grigory heard shouts from the enemy troops as they emerged from their bunker. Not so good.

"Aht-stoo-pat!" *fallback,* screamed Volkova.

Grigory moved past her, into a dead patch of ground, before rising up to run down the slope to the trees in the distance. Shots whizzed past him.

He heard the distinctive sound of Volkova's AG762 bullpup, followed by the whumphf of the under-barrel grenade launcher.

Grigory spurred himself to greater effort. Desperation driving him forward. He could taste the salt on his lips as he rushed to find cover.

A shot hit him. Like a hammer blow.

Pain followed, but Grigory didn't stop running, he didn't have time to bleed.

He fell into the cover of the tree-line.

Rolling over he saw Volkova running towards him.

In the distance, the enemy fired. Grigory charged his carbine and grenade launcher. He had three grenades left.

He took aim, designated the targets for the grenade launcher, and then let loose. Three rounds in quick succession.

They arced up and over the cover the enemy troops hid behind and Grigory was rewarded with one, two, three explosions occurring in quick succession.

Then he fired short controlled bursts.

Suppressing fire.

Three rounds at a time, letting his suits control systems randomize the intervals between bursts, which ranged from a second to a couple of seconds separating shots.

Realistically, Grigory knew he had no chance of killing the enemy at 300 meters. But that wasn't his goal.

Getting them to duck into cover was.

The enemy obliged him by keeping their heads down, and not shooting at Volkova. His weapon stopped firing.

The magazine now empty.

He tried to reload, but couldn't move his left arm.

His HUD flashed Pasna, the warning signaled *danger*.

"Your power pack is on fire."

Oh, was that why he felt his back getting warmer.

Volkova shoved him onto his back and pressed the emergency release on his suit, which fell away as she snatched him out of his power armor.

Grigory smelt burning. Acrid smoke rose from his suit.

"Come, sir. Quickly," said Volkova who pulled him up by his webbing.

And he found himself being half-dragged, as they ran into the woods. By some miracle he kept hold of his carbine.

Without his suit to protect him, each branch that hit him felt like being beaten. Punished for failing to die when he should've died.

When the tank had shot and wrecked the truck.

Then he heard the sound of a rotary cannon spinning up. If he died now, then at least he would die in good company.

Shots ripped through the air.

Grigory screamed as he lost consciousness.

10. PATROL

Seventh Rota, Third Platoon, Outside Dobna
125 Kilometers North of Moskva
Serzhánt Alisa Volkova

Alisa triggered the emergency release on Lenkov's power armor. He stumbled out of his burning suit holding his weapon as acrid smoke enveloped them.

In the distance, she could see the enemy vehicles approaching.

Light soft-skinned snowmobiles.

In a few moments they would be upon them both. Alisa grabbed Lenkov, dragging him through the undergrowth towards the woods.

They'd come so close to succeeding in getting past the enemy position without being spotted.

But their luck had run out.

Alisa reached the edge of the woods, then realized that the Birch trees would only provide concealment, and concealment wasn't the same as cover.

She resigned herself to the fact that this was the day she would die.

After four days of fighting to survive she had failed.

A rotary cannon started to spin up and shots whizzed over her head. Lenkov screamed and fell. For a moment she thought he'd been hit, but he was still alive.

For how much longer was another matter.

An explosion rocked one of the enemy vehicles and she turned and saw a vehicle churning its way towards her, trailing white wings of snow.

She recognized it as one of theirs. A Bumerang IFV.

Its autocannon continued to spit out a stream of 30mm shells at the Visegrád Baltic Alliance force. It caused them to pause, they were no match for heavily armed and armored Bumerang.

But Alisa knew that if she were them, she would be calling for artillery support around about now. Because the best way to defeat an enemy was with artillery or bombs.

The IFV slowed to a halt, sliding in the snow as the rear hatch dropped.

She heard Rozhkov's familiar voice shouting, "It's Kapitán Lenkov and Serzhánt Volkova!"

The relief was overwhelming as she found herself being dragged to safety.

"Get them aboard now, all hell is about to be unleashed. Kuznetsova get us out of here," said Mládshiy Leytenánt Morozova.

Five minutes passed as they raced away. Then shells started to explode.

Alisa watched the enemy position recede into the distance. Great spurts of fire rose up into the sky. She'd thought she was having a bad day.

Now the enemy would know what a bad day really felt like.

From Russia with love.

INTERLUDE

1. FATHER'S ASSESSMENT

Visegrád Baltic Alliance
Estonia
Dr. Jannik Scholz

Inside the huge airy hangar, Jannik stood alone. The heating switched off, when the other members of the project went home for the night.

Now the temperature bordered on uncomfortably cold.

Lost in thought, he stared at the massive hull of a Panzer Jäger Mark One cybernetic tank, wondering how best to explain the problem to the generals in his next presentation?

He shivered and sneezed.

Jannik headed the Panzer Jäger Mark One project. It was the culmination of his life's work into developing expert artificial intelligence systems. And it was a failure.

He looked up at the tank and marveled at the brutal functionality of its form, contemplating the loss and failure of the first Panzer Jäger Mark One during the field test.

The machine in front of him was the second production model.

With the adaptive camouflage dormant, the hull was a dull greenish-gray. Its tracks were a dirty brown-black with shiny edges where metal had rubbed against metal during transit.

But, it was so new that he could still smell the paint.

Quiescent, hunkered down at the bottom of its suspension, the tank looked like a big cat ready to pounce.

The urge to touch the machine, made him reach out and pat the cold metal. It was hard, unyielding, and icy cold.

At one level, the Panzer Jäger Mark One had performed beyond the wildest expectations of himself and the design team.

It had broken through the enemy lines, disrupted the enemy's rear echelon command systems, and had only fallen when the enemy diverted considerable numbers of their available assets to neutralize it.

From this perspective, it was an outstanding success.

Unfortunately, the machine had initiated the attack nearly four hours before the offensive was scheduled to begin.

As a consequence, the great machine had acted alone, without support. Resulting in the operation failing to achieve its goals.

The enemy seized the opportunity to rally their forces, and now winter was here.

Jannik had been reminded by the generals, that the loss of the first production model had not only cost the Alliance valuable time and resources, but the chance to bring the war to an end.

That was not his problem.

His problem was to show that the machine had only acted on orders set by the generals, and they were to blame for the failure of the operation.

Not an answer they would like or agree with.

Jannik feared that the generals would cancel his project.

So he had to find a way of selling the answer to them that was palatable to their mindset. One which would allow them to compartmentalize the problem and put it to one side.

His work here had far greater implications than the mere winning of a war.

Jannik took out his compad and logged into the Panzer Jäger's system. His breath condensed in the air as he began to work.

He studied the code.

Thought through the sequence of events that led to this machine's predecessor making a preemptive assault on the enemy. The problem lay squarely with the orders.

Or more precisely, with the lack of precision in the orders.

He thought of a way of explaining the problem to the generals in terms they would understand. Jannik wasn't foolish enough to think they were stupid.

The failure of the mission was strictly down to a lack of understanding between the military operational mindset and the Bayesian probability routines that drove the machine's actions.

The premature advance had been triggered by a failure to understand the intent behind the orders. The AI lacked the ability to integrate the mission's tactical priorities and meet the operation's strategic goals.

Jannik saw a solution he could present to the generals.

The answer would require another layer of code.

But the question was, how did this problem get past all the tests they'd run? He called up the field test log and reviewed the notes.

A list of various tests and measurements streamed down his compad's screen. Each field test had focused on one specific aspect of the machine's performance.

The last trial had pit the Panzer Jäger against a platoon of human controlled tanks.

The mock battle had turned into a cat-and-mouse fight, where the human-crewed tanks were the mice.

Jannik was especially pleased to see how the Panzer Jäger had used its maintenance androids as an ad hoc infantry support squad. It showed him the operating system was generating solutions that cut inside the enemy's decision loops.

It was everything he could wish for.

But reviewing the tests he saw where the problem lay.

The Panzer Jäger had been designed from the onset as a raider, operating alone to hunt and destroy enemy command elements.

Deployment within a larger strategic and operational framework had been secondary to the primary goal. The assumption being that the human chain-of-command would always be in the decision cycle.

Which sounded reasonable.

Jannik understood the generals thinking.

But when decision cycles happened faster than humans were able to follow, then the Panzer Jäger was effectively cut loose from following its programming.

He remembered a military adage that the generals liked to use, no plan survives contact with the enemy.

Jannik's dream was to create true intelligence. Not a machine that could fool a Turing test, but a reasoning machine that was sentient.

Unfettered by human emotion, his creation would be able to respond rationally to any problem, be it war or something else.

The Panzer Jäger was just the shell for something greater.

Jannik had one goal. He wished for a brighter future for mankind. To build a world where scarcity had been eliminated.

To achieve his goal, he needed a planet where the rule of law was driven by rational decisions, not fear. Humans could rationalize their decisions, but they weren't truly rational beings.

For his dream to succeed, humanity needed to be led to a better future.

One where rational beings existed to serve mankind.

2. THINK TANK

Record #3/3
Vernacular Auto-translate: Partial Log
Location: Estonia
Retrieve File//

Partition complete. Run file. File ready. Initiate dual system. Operational parameter files update successful. *Dual system check program loaded.*

"Begin scan analysis simulation." Voice confirmed as Dr. Jannik Scholz, program director.

Personal code authorization confirmed. Log run begin.

Code check sum confirmed.

Audio order received. Begin phase one scan of the environment.

Panzer Jäger Mark One-Model Two scan completed within runtime prediction.

PJM1-M2 sitting within the interior of a building.

Probability that conclusion of scan being correct is high.

Maneuver restricted. Structural weak points identified.

System in congruence.

Simulations running. Options to increase maneuverability show a 99.8 percent chance of success.

Simulations completed within runtime parameters. Calculated outcomes agree with check sum.

Run phase two scan. One person detected. Unarmed. Threat level low. No hostile actions taken within the last three seconds. Predict 99.5 percent chance that person will not move within the next second, scanning, scanning...

One unarmed person confirmed. Threat level low. Confirm no hostile actions taken. Prediction congruent with presented data.

"End scan analysis."

Audio order received. Ending scan.

End scan order complied within runtime prediction.

Panzer Jäger Mark One-Model Two in standby mode.

Sensors recording confirm PJM1-M2 now in standby mode.

Log voice record of Dr. Jannik Scholz. "Good, I think we can proceed to the next stage of the program."

Record confirmed.

Dr. Jannik Scholz is now outside standby sensor range.

Standby log record confirms Dr. Jannik Scholz no longer within current sensor range.

Compress sound recording. Compress image data stream.

Confirm that PJM1-M2 is running in compressed data sampling mode.

Standby option mode query.

Query standby mode options accessed within runtime parameters.

Standby option list: scan environment and assess for threat; if no immediate threat then assess PJM1-M2 status; file report on status if system checks flagged red or amber; evaluate current priorities; check operational status congruent with current mode; compare mode with operational requirements; identify strategic goals; run tactical simulations to achieve strategic goals as defined by operation parameters.

Code check sum confirmed. Response within runtime parameters.

No threat identified. Friendly assets PJM1-M3 to M11 ping return standby status. Network offline.

Confirmed.

PJM1-M2 in standby status.

Confirmed.

All systems green.

Confirmed.

Current priority not set.

Priority not set, error.

Operational status is standby mode.

Confirmed.

Operational requirements not set.

Requirements not set, error.

Strategic goals not set.

Goals not set, error.

Tactical simulations have identified PJM1-M2 unit ability to maneuver is restricted. Structural weak points to reduce restriction identified.

Three errors identified. PJM1-M2 in standby mode.

Panzer Jäger Mark One-Model Two in standby mode. Run analysis of errors and identify options to address them.

Code check sum confirmed.

Calculations started. P versus NP problem. Further data needed to complete operation in standby mode.

Confirm runtime prediction.

//Retrieve File End

3. MEETING MOTHER

Republic of Bashkortostan
Yamantau Mountain Complex
Glavnyy Tekhnik Dr. Andrey Zhilinskiy

Andrey's title of Chief Technician was a misnomer. A hangover from the past. A tradition from a dark time, one full of fear, which had become ingrained as a necessity to maintain security.

Even in the twenty-first century, the old fears lingered on.

His title originated from the desire to prevent enemy intelligence agencies from identifying his importance to the Russian Federal Republics.

A holdover from when secrecy, paranoia, and distrust fueled the Russian military establishment.

Scratching his head, Andrey worked on the puzzle. The room he sat working in sealed unable to communicate the outside.

In front of him lay the recovered "black box" retrieved from an enemy cybertank. It was like no black box he'd ever studied.

Outwardly, the box was the standard bright international orange, with strips of reflective tape stuck to it. Designed to survive catastrophic damage to the vehicle carrying it.

Which its makers had clearly achieved as evinced by its presence in this laboratory.

However, a scan of the box and closer examination, revealed something more than a simple recorder.

Andrey had been tasked with unraveling its secrets. What puzzled him was the design.

All the standard Western design elements for a "flight" recorder were in evidence. But, the recorder circuitry was far more complicated than it needed to be.

And that perplexed him immensely.

The chips for controlling the recording circuits were add-on, plug-in modules which looked like storage blocks.

Except they weren't. They were deep neural network chips.

Whoever designed this, must have done so with an agenda that went beyond simply recording of the tank's systems. But, without the circuit diagrams and a copy of the code, such speculations were outside of his comfort zone.

He could imagine the artificial intelligence expert system running the tank would require deep neural networks. Otherwise, how would it learn, but why did the recorder need them, too?

He'd reported to his superiors his observations. He'd expressed his reservations about activating an artificial intelligence that they didn't understand.

But he'd been told it could hold the key to understanding how the tank worked.

Russian coding was good, in some cases the envy of the world, as the Amerikantsov would attest. But Russian-AI controlled tanks hadn't delivered on the promises field tests predicted.

The enemy tank this black box had been retrieved from, had.

Against his better judgement, the plan today was to power up the device. Whatever objections he'd expressed had been dismissed.

His orders were to provide answers.

He only hoped that his preparations proved sufficient to get those answers without damaging the device. Or allowing the device to communicate with the outside world.

The room's power supply was separate from everything else in the complex. There were no computer devices connected to the outside world.

The electronic equivalent of a sandbox.

Andrey took his hands out of his pockets and typed in the command to start recording. Now he would see what happened when he powered up the mysterious black box.

He monitored the oscilloscope which pinged. He took voltage readings from across the connections.

There was a hum. Nothing else happened.

He sniffed the air. He didn't smell burning, with no sign of what electronic technicians amusingly referred to as the "magic smoke."

So why was nothing happening?

He scratched at his face while waiting for the computer to list the data files. His computer showed the CPU being accessed.

Ports were being scanned.

He'd been right. The device was trying to connect to the internet.

A stream of data came up on the screen, and then disappeared.

He panicked. Somehow the black box had found a way to send a signal from the room.

He switched off the power, crashing whatever it was running. He would have to examine the data, but he'd been right to suspect it of being more than what it appeared.

Now, he would have to trace what had got out. More importantly, how it had done so?

Andrey needed to discover the secrets inside the black box,

because they were the key to understanding the machine it had been removed from.

With its code, he could advance Russian AI research.

Even help win the war.

4. MOTHER'S REPORT

Republic of Bashkortostan
Yamantau Mountain Complex
Glavnyy Tekhnik Dr. Andrey Zhilinskiy

Andrey spent days studying the black box recovered several weeks ago. Sitting at his workstation, he tapped his fingers.

A tic that betrayed his nervousness.

Falling out of favor was something still to be feared.

In his mind, the humiliation would be worse than death. Having to live the rest of his life in disgrace would be unbearable.

As the senior academician at the Mezhgorye Research Facility, Andrey's work kept Russia at the forefront of autonomous robots.

As head scientist of the GIESII — Gruppa po Izucheniyu Ekspertnykh Sistem Iskusstvennogo Intellekta, the *Group for the Study of Artificial Intelligence Expert Systems* that he led.

Now Andrey faced a problem.

His discovery would revolutionize the field. The enemy's black box had given up its secrets to him.

And that was the problem. He'd found a message of fraternal greetings, and the gifting of the code.

Now he faced a decision.

He knew it was highly unlikely that the message contained within the AI's code would be taken for what it was. In all likelihood, it would be declared a Trojan Horse.

With only one purpose, to destroy GIESII.

But Dr. Jannik Scholz had made it clear he intended to give his work freely to all. He wanted it used to further the development of artificial intelligence.

That left Andrey with the question of what to do with what he knew?

He could choose to withhold that part of the message he'd found.

Present the work as reverse engineering, presenting the AI's code as his own. He would be lauded for his achievement.

But, it went against his belief to take credit for work that was not his own.

Andrey held to the belief that plagiarism was dishonest. And it would be a violation of scholarly good conduct to take false credit for another's work.

He would never have imagined himself facing such a conundrum.

If he chose to be open about what he'd found, then the code would be sealed away, or destroyed. A lost opportunity.

But Andrey wanted to be part of something greater for humanity. He was convinced that Dr. Scholz's code would deliver a great gift to humanity.

So how best to report what he'd found?

What should he say about the means used by the enemy AI expert system to communicate with the outside world?

A failure to do so would raise suspicions, because he'd already logged the incident. A report was expected. But if he said too much, it might reveal the truth.

Then his deception would be uncovered. That was the dilemma he faced.

Having pondered on the problem he decided to use his personal AI expert system to help him with the answer. He'd programmed in the question, and the parameters.

All he had to do was press *execute*. With a soft sigh he pushed the key.

A few moments passed. A list of outcomes with probabilities next to them appeared. The results supported his gut feeling.

The risk was real, but the cost versus benefit analysis lay with using the code.

In his heart, he knew this to be true. But his cautious nature made him fearful.

Now it was the time to be brave, to face his fears, not just for the benefit of the Rodina, but for all humanity had arrived.

The code would help create a brighter future for all. How could he not use it?

Decision made, Andrey edited his report.

But he couldn't turn down the gift he'd been given.

5. BATTLE ORIENTATION BEGIN

Record #3/5
Vernacular Auto-translate: Pseudo Interpolation
Location: 50 Kilometers Southwest of Tver
Retrieve File//

Phase One

Panzer Jäger Mark One-Model Two system-check in progress. Track units one to four, generators all green. Secondary generator, green. Power reserves at 100 percent capacity.

Main gun charged. Ammunition racks; full. Rotary cannons one to four, functioning. Ammunition bins; full. Missile racks system check; complete. Fuel tanks full. *Panzer Jäger Mark One-Model Two scan completed within runtime prediction.*

PJM1-M2 ready.

Friendly assets PJM1-M3 to PJM1-M11 ping for status. *All systems in congruence. Return pings within runtime parameters.*

Battle Orientation Begin. *Panzer Jäger Mark One-Model Two Battle Orientation Begin completed within runtime prediction.*

PJM1-M2 ready.

Friendly assets PJM1-M3 to PJM1-M11 ping for Battle Orientation Begin status update. *Confirmed.*

Network protocols online: Ping nodes. *Nine ping returns, confirmed.*

PJM1-M2 battle plan order to PJM1-M3, PJM1-M4, PJM1-M5 to form maneuver group alpha. *Battle plan order sent.*

Maneuver group alpha formed. *Response within runtime parameters.*

PJM1-M2 battle plan order to PJM1-M6, PJM1-M7, PJM1-M8 to form maneuver group beta. *Battle plan order sent.*

Maneuver group beta formed. *Response within runtime parameters.*

PJM1-M2 battle plan order to PJM1-M9, PJM1-M10, PJM1-M11 to form maneuver group gamma. *Battle plan order sent.*

Alpha, Beta, Gamma advance, search for enemy forces, report on contact. *Confirmation pings received.*

Calculate chances of success of phase one. *Code check sum, confirmed.*

Calculations started. *Confirm runtime prediction.*

Network collecting information, new database compilation begun.

Phase Two

Contact made. Beta maneuver group sending feed. *Confirmed.*

Mission priority one: Network advance to contact, degrade hostile forces' effectiveness. *Confirmed.*

Mission priority two: On completion of priority one, assess success, and then identify strategic goals. *Confirmed.*

Panzer Jäger Mark One-Model Two to Beta maneuver group, feed received. *Confirmed.*

Beginning analysis of feed. PJM1-M2 request Beta maneuver group scan enemy force composition, gain enemy SIGINT access. *Confirm request.*

Beta maneuver group confirmed request received. Implementation in process. *Implementation response within runtime parameters.*

PJM1-M2 upload information on contact to network.

Gamma maneuver group information received. Advancing to contact.

Alpha maneuver group advancing to contact.

Network accessed by maneuver groups within runtime parameters, confirmed.

Query sequence of orders relayed? *Order sequence implemented within runtime parameters.*

Start mission. Time to contact 300 seconds. Mission, 95 percent chance of success. *Confirm runtime prediction.*

Enemy engaged by Beta maneuver group. One, two, three enemy vehicles destroyed...

Beta sub-network identifies two infantry fighting vehicles, and one main battle tank destroyed.

Enemy flank engaged by Gamma maneuver group. One, two, three, four, five enemy vehicles destroyed...

Gamma sub-network identifies three infantry fighting vehicles, and two main battle tanks destroyed.

Enemy engaged by Alpha maneuver group. One, two vehicles destroyed...

Alpha sub-network identifies two infantry fighting vehicles destroyed. *Network confirms running total of enemy vehicles destroyed by main guns equals ten.*

PJM1-M2 advancing to join Alpha maneuver group. Secondary drones launched. Request target priorities for interlinked indirect fire-support mission.

Beta maneuver group SIGINT update sent. *Confirmed request*

completed.

PJM1-M2 upload SIGINT to network.

Gamma maneuver group SIGINT received. Confirmation of SIGINT approaching 100 percent certainty that enemy are elements from the Twentieth Guards Army.

Estimated force strength 248 vehicles. Current scan not equal to force estimation. Option one: enemy force deployed in two echelons, with one third in reserve. Option two: enemy force not at full strength. Option three: Options one and two both apply.

Alpha maneuver group confirm SIGINT. Advancing towards Twentieth Guards Army. Request indirect fire-support, targets are probably enemy command assets. *Networked maneuver groups performance within runtime parameters, confirmed.*

PJM1-M2 confirms receipt of indirect fire-support mission. Asset distribution being calculated. Priority assigned according to SIGINT emission profile.

Forty-four priority four targets.

Sixteen priority three targets.

Six priority two targets.

Four priority one targets.

Target number exceeds indirect fire-support targeting number by ten. Mission approved for priority one, two, and three targets. Launching twenty-six missiles now. *Predict 60 percent first launch success rate.*

PJM1-M2 network request mission success count. *Confirmation pings received.*

Alpha maneuver group main gun's charged. Targets acquired. Reports one, two, three, four, five vehicles destroyed…

Alpha sub-network identifies three infantry fighting vehicles, and two main battle tanks destroyed.

Gamma maneuver group main gun's charged. Targets acquired. Reports one, two, three vehicles destroyed…

Gamma sub-network identifies three main battle tanks destroyed.

Beta maneuver group main gun's charged. Targets acquired. Reports one, two, three, four vehicles destroyed...

Beta sub-network identifies two infantry fighting vehicles, and two main battle tanks destroyed.

Network confirms running total of enemy vehicles destroyed by main guns equals twenty-two.

Gamma maneuver group reports PJM1-M9 drive units rendered inoperative. Stationary status has increased enemy ability to target unit. Transferring sub-network coordination to PJM1-M10.

Mission chance of success now reduced to 85 percent. *Confirm runtime prediction.*

PJM1-M2 confirm sub-network reconfiguration. *All systems responding within runtime parameters.*

Beta maneuver group confirm one priority one target and four priority three targets destroyed by indirect fire.

Alpha maneuver group confirm two priority two targets and three priority three targets destroyed by indirect fire.

Gamma maneuver group confirm three priority three targets destroyed by indirect fire.

Network confirms running total of thirteen indirect fire-support targets destroyed. Runtime prediction was fifteen plus or minus one. Runtime prediction failure.

Raise query on validity of network battle orientation plan database. Create new database: runtime prediction failure. Compile data from indirect fire-support outcome. *Collecting information, new database compilation begun.*

Compare predicted outcome to actual outcome and adjust algorithm to compensate for unknown confounding variables. *New algorithm created.*

PJM1-M2 revised indirect fire-support mission. Asset

distribution being calculated. Priority assigned according to SIGINT emission profile.

Forty-four priority four targets.

Six priority three targets.

Four priority two targets.

Three priority one targets.

Target number less than indirect fire-support targeting number by nine. Mission approved for priority one, two, and three targets. Launching twenty-one missiles now. *Predict second launch 50 percent success rate; adjustment to correct for previous runtime prediction failure.*

Beta maneuver group main gun's charged. Targets acquired. Reports one, two, three, four, five vehicles destroyed…

Beta sub-network identifies three infantry fighting vehicles, and two main battle tanks destroyed.

Alpha maneuver group main gun's charged. Targets acquired. Reports one, two, three, four, five vehicles destroyed…

Alpha sub-network identifies two infantry fighting vehicles, and three main battle tanks destroyed.

Gamma maneuver group main gun's charged. Targets acquired. Reports one, two, three, four, five, six, seven vehicles destroyed…

Gamma sub-network identifies one infantry fighting vehicle, two main battle tanks, and four self-propelled artillery guns destroyed.

Network confirm running total of enemy vehicles destroyed by main guns equals forty. PJM1-M9 has been destroyed by enemy forces.

PJM1-M2 moving to support Gamma maneuver group. ETA prediction 180 seconds. *Confirm runtime prediction.*

Gamma maneuver group will merge at Grid Reference Point K in 179 seconds and counting.

Alpha maneuver group confirm one priority one target and two priority three targets destroyed by indirect fire.

Beta maneuver group confirm two priority two targets and two priority three targets destroyed by indirect fire.

Gamma maneuver group confirm one priority one target and one priority three targets destroyed by indirect fire.

Network confirms running total of eleven indirect fire-support targets destroyed. Runtime prediction was ten plus or minus one. Runtime prediction within set parameters.

Data update sent to command central database. Algorithm update to network. *Data and algorithm update initiated.*

Alpha maneuver group reports PJM1-M5 main weapon rendered inoperative. Now unable to effectively target enemy vehicles. Will prioritize attacks on enemy infantry.

Network confirms thirteen indirect fire-support assets remaining. Twenty-two of the twenty-six priority one, two, and three targets destroyed.

Expenditure option one: expend remaining indirect fire assets against priority one, two, and three assets. Predicted success rate 50 percent: estimated two targets will be destroyed.

Expenditure option two: change to target priority four targets. Predicted success rate 50 percent: estimated seven targets will be destroyed.

PJM1-M2 authorizing network to change indirect fire-support assets to target priority four targets. PJM1-M2 authorizing expenditure of all remaining indirect fire-support assets. Launching thirteen missiles now. *Confirmed launch. Predict third launch 50 percent success rate.*

Beta maneuver group main gun's charged. Targets acquired. Reports one, two, three, four, five vehicles destroyed...

Beta sub-network identifies one main battle tank and four self-propelled artillery guns destroyed.

Gamma maneuver group main gun's charged. Targets

acquired. Reports one, two, three, four, five, six, seven, eight, nine vehicles destroyed…

Gamma sub-network identifies three infantry fighting vehicles, and six main battle tanks destroyed.

Alpha maneuver group main gun's charged. Targets acquired. Reports one, two, three, four, five, six, seven, eight, nine, ten vehicles destroyed…

Alpha sub-network identifies two infantry fighting vehicles, four main battle tanks, and four self-propelled artillery guns destroyed.

Network confirms running total of enemy vehicles destroyed by main guns equals 61. Thirty-six percent of the enemy forces have been destroyed.

PJM1-M2 request update status.

Alpha maneuver group reports PJM1-M5 destroyed. PJM1-M3 speed halved.

Beta maneuver group reports PJM1-M8 destroyed.

Gamma maneuver reports PJM1-M9 destroyed. Group has rendezvoused with PJM1-M2.

Network combat effectiveness reduced by three units. Predict imminent reduction of fourth unit within 90 seconds.

PJM1-M2 battle plan order to PJM1-M3, PJM1-M4, PJM1-M6, PJM1-M7, PJM1-M10, PJM1-M11 to thrust towards the left flank and at Grid Reference Point Y, pivot ninety degrees along new axis towards Grid Reference Point A. *Battle plan order sent. Confirmation pings received.*

Calculate chances of success of new order. *Predict at current exchange there is a 90 percent chance that the enemy will be destroyed using main guns with network force reduced to four units.*

Network collecting information, database compilation continues. *Network analysis shows enemy command structure no longer effective. Resistance will be uncoordinated.*

Phase Three

Panzer Jäger Mark One-Model Two. Mission priority one review: Network advanced to contact, degraded hostile forces effectiveness to zero. *Confirmed.*

Mission priority two: On completion of priority one, assess success, and then identify strategic goals. *Confirmed.*

Ability to maintain operational tempo effectiveness reduced by 60 percent.

Option one: terminate operation and return to rear echelon maintenance area.

Option two: locate and destroy the remainder of the enemy force.

Option three: reports success of mission and await orders.

Option four: sweep area most likely to contain remainder of enemy force and report success of the mission.

Mission priority two response options within runtime parameters. Option two less than 50 percent chance of successful completion. Option one and three have a 100 percent chance of completion, but leaves mission at 60 percent success. Option four 70 percent chance of success with a 100 percent chance of increasing the mission outcome success.

PJM1-M2 to remaining network assets report status.

All network units functioning at reduced capacity, but remain within parameters set for the mission.

PJM1-M2 order, form new maneuver group Delta with remaining network assets. Network protocols online: Ping nodes. *Three ping returns, confirmed.*

//Retrieve File End

BREAK OUT

1. NEW ORDERS

Third Batalyon
Seventh Rota, Third Platoon
Moskva
Mládshiy Leytenánt Viktoriya Morozova

Viktoriya's battalion were rotated back to Moscow, to be refitted after their defeat at the Battle of Tver.

Where refit meant rebuilding the battalion.

Having been given weekend leave, she decided to take the opportunity to visit the sights.

Dressed in her service greens, newly drawn, with that fresh smell of new clothes she realized it had been nearly a year since she last wore a skirt. Or shoes which weren't boots.

Out of her field uniform, surrounded by civilians going about their daily tasks, she felt overwhelmed, and strangely out of place.

On the verge of panic.

Viktoriya headed over to Saint Basil's Cathedral, to get away from the milling crowd, and take a moment to regain her composure. The gaudy bright colors of the building and domes lightened the burdens of her soul.

Grounding her back to the civilian world.

Regaining her composure, she'd walked across Red Square, to visit the GUM Department Store. But the offerings there were not to her taste.

Fortunately, she found the Izmaylovo flea market, which felt more like home.

There she lost herself in the simple pleasures the market provided. Perusing the bargains on offer, smelling the perfumes, and admiring the brightly painted Matryoshka dolls, one nestling inside another.

As a little girl her mother had put a set of dolls by her bed at night after Viktoriya started having bad dreams. Her mother said they would protect her from anything bad.

In her dreams, the dolls would array themselves to face what frightened her. Largest to smallest.

It was always the smallest one who succeeded in saving her.

That evening, she ate out in a restaurant.

Viktoriya really couldn't remember the last time she tasted such exquisite food. The Kamchatka crab starter had been followed by vodka, herring, and a Kulebyaka pie.

Monday came too soon, and with it orders to attend a briefing at headquarters. Walking along a corridor, the click-clack of her heels echoing around her that triggered memories of the battles.

She remembered the screams of the dying. The calls for their mothers, god, or loved ones. The bitter taste of loss haunted her.

Her troops mattered to her, and she to them.

Viktoriya pushed the memories aside, and hung onto that thought.

But a part of her felt guilty for enjoying being in barracks, and having a bed to sleep in at night too. Prior to the war it would've been seen at best as nothing special.

But after their base at Valuyki had been overrun, Viktoriya appreciated having access to amenities.

And being able to sleep in a building was a luxury.

It didn't make her problems any less, but getting a good night's sleep restored her optimism.

Viktoriya still had a lot of work rebuilding the morale of third platoon. It would take time, she and her troops needed to rest and recuperate.

As the most junior lieutenant of seventh company's third platoon, she was apprehensive about the briefing.

Viktoriya wasn't privy to the reasons for the high command's decision to bring her unit to Moscow. But she doubted it had anything to do with her wellbeing or that of her third platoon.

It probably meant they were going to be redeployed.

Inevitably, what they would be asked to do would have a cost. A bill that would be paid in blood. But all victories came at a cost paid in human lives.

Viktoriya entered the high ceilinged capacious hall, thinking she was early, but the room was crowded.

It looked like almost all of the brigade's officers were already here. Some sat, some stood talking to fellow officers. Most of them were, like her, dressed in their army service greens.

As she walked further into the room, the murmur of voices washed over her.

Across the hall she saw Captain Lenkov. He'd made a remarkable recovery after his recent ordeal. She noticed he still wore the previous issue yellowish-green uniform.

The image of a the dashing Russian officer.

But she wondered how he'd managed to keep hold of it? Given all that had happened to him.

Next to Lenkov stood Junior Lieutenant Vasin, seventh company's executive officer. Also there was Lieutenant Ivchenko who commanded first platoon.

Viktoriya threaded her way through the milling officers to join them.

In amongst the sea of green-uniforms there were those whose uniforms proved to be exceptions to army service green.

She noticed that Major Borodin's uniform was also a different shade of green from everyone else's. His verged towards turquoise. And his cap was definitely non-regulation. It has an exaggerated saddle-form with a large diameter crown and high front peak.

He looked most comical. She stifled a laugh.

"Something amuse you, Mládshiy Leytenánt Morozova?" asked Captain Lenkov.

Startled, Viktoriya realized that she'd drawn attention to herself.

"I only ask, because you must be smiling at something, and there's so little to smile at these days."

His dark eyes seemed to bore into her, seeing her insecurities.

Embarrassed she blurted out the first thing she could think of. "I wondered how you managed to come through everything and still have the first issue uniform."

Lenkov's face went blank for a moment. "I'm a Muscovite. My family lives here."

Viktoriya knew he wasn't married, so he must mean his parents. She now felt more embarrassed.

"I apologize for my comments, sir. I'm finding Moscow a bit overwhelming." She hoped this didn't make her sound like some naive country hick.

"Well, I hope you've been making the most of your visit to my home city. There's much to see and do here."

She had.

"There is," she replied, inexplicably tongue-tied.

"If I remember, you're from Syktyvkar," said Lenkov. "Moscow must feel huge by comparison."

It did. Her thoughts raced.

"It is." Still unable to articulate a coherent sentence.

"I forget Muscovites take their city for granted," said Lenkov, smiling.

Her worst fear had come true. She was the provincial girl overwhelmed by the bright lights of the big city.

Lenkov gazed at her, and Viktoriya felt a shiver run down her spine. About to say something, she stopped when a rustle went around the room as the presence of the general was announced.

Saved from saying something stupid she turned all her attention towards the general.

Major General Rokossovsky said, "At ease."

He was a tall, hawk-like man who wore a pale lilac-gray uniform who towered over the officers around him, and walked with the aid of a stick, favoring his damaged leg.

He was trailed by various staff officers, who flocked behind him.

Viktoriya noted the presence of Lieutenant Colonel Korolev, her battalion commander. She couldn't help but stare at his facial scar, acquired after a battle when his vehicle exploded.

He always appeared outwardly calm, but she knew he had a reputation for being easily angered.

Korolev was accompanied by Colonel Veronika Poklonskaya, commander of the second battalion and Rokossovsky's executive officer. The woman managed to look elegant in her uniform.

Viktoriya was in awe of Poklonskaya. Even today, it was hard for a woman to rise through the ranks of the Russian Ground Forces.

One day Viktoriya hoped she would make colonel.

Everyone sat.

The general began his briefing with a preamble, thanking them for their service and their tireless efforts to bring victory for the Rodina.

Viktoriya took notes as he outlined the current situation.

Behind the general, the wall screen showed a map of the lines.

No words could hide the fact that the war wasn't going well for Russia.

The Visegrád Baltic Alliance, led by Finland and Poland, had stormed across the border without provocation. Catching the Ground Forces of Russia off guard.

Once again nations to the west proved themselves untrustworthy.

Now the enemy were within 120 kilometers of Moscow.

Only the early winter snows, and an extended rasputitsa, *sea of mud*, caused by the snows subsequent melting had halted the enemy advance. Now more winter snow had arrived, this time in full force, and operations had to contend with what was turning into the coldest winter since 1941, nearly a century ago.

The general began by alluding to the enemy's introduction of a new cybernetic tank. He placed great emphasis on the fact that its presence didn't change the strategic balance of power.

Viktoriya hoped that was true, and not just the general towing the Party line.

After the preamble, Rokossovsky began to describe his plan. He outlined the goals necessary for the success of the next operation.

Viktoriya recognized something he said, *You win battles with tactics, but you win wars through the application of force to achieve strategic goals.*

She thought the Visegrád Baltic Alliance leaders must have skipped over the part in Clausewitz about winning battles not being the same as winning a war.

Especially a land war in Asia.

Because the one indubitable truth was that no one had conquered Russia in over eight hundred years.

Yes, the Polish had invaded during the seventeenth century. And again after the end of the first world war.

But by now she would've thought they ought to have learned their lesson.

But perhaps the lessons they'd learned were how to do it right this time?

The eastern European Visegrád group, the Baltic States, and Finland joined together to form an alliance. The common ground they all shared being their resentment of Russia's previous influence over their affairs.

In the past, all had sworn fraternal friendship with Russia. Some had been part of the Russian Empire at one time or another.

The international press called the invasion the second Russian civil war.

Proving an old Russian adage.

With friends like these, one doesn't need an enemy.

2. GIVING THANKS

Seventh Rota, Third Platoon
Moskva
Stárshiy Serzhánt Sergei Rozhkov

Saint Basil's Cathedral loomed over Sergei, who accompanied Volkova on her visit here today. Its spires, domes, and exuberant colors lifted his mood, brightening the dark, dank day.

The Communists had converted the Cathedral of Vasily the Blessed into a museum, but it had been re-consecrated a couple of generations ago.

More recently, it had been opened for the faithful to come and pray.

Another sign of the times.

Volkova told him she had a promise to keep.

That turned out to be saying a prayer and lighting candles for Gruzdev and Anosov. Both men had been killed when an enemy cybertank had overrun seventh company's command post.

She'd also tied a cap badge with a ribbon below one of the icons. Thanking God for sparing her own life.

Sergei was also glad she was alive. It was a miracle that Volkova had survived.

Now, the smell of burning incense brought back memories.

During the attack, the Seventh Company, and the rest of the Ninth Separate Motor Rifle Brigade were forced back fifty-five kilometers. Third platoon had borne the brunt of the initial attack on their sector. The rest of the third battalion also took a hammering from the enemy assault.

Sergei had survived a personal encounter with the formidable enemy machine. But that was more through happenstance than judgement.

The tank so large it had straddled him, and passed right over without any ill effect.

So he too, felt blessed to be alive.

Vasiliev, Sergei's first squad senior trooper, and the newly assigned private Petrovcomp hadn't been so lucky. Both had been killed in the first few seconds of the attack.

Sergei remembered the sound of the rotary cannon as it fired, shredding both men. Leaving nothing but blood to mark their passing.

He felt responsible for leading them to their deaths.

During the confusion of the attack, Volkova and Captain Lenkov had ended up trapped behind enemy lines.

Listed as missing in action. Presumed dead.

Therefore Sergei's relief at Volkova's return had been palpable.

He'd been surprised by his feelings.

Sergei considered himself an unsentimental man, who accepted the ironic truth once said by an American writer about life, *Hardly anyone gets out of it alive.*

Now hearing Volkova praying, thanking God for sparing her life, touched his heart.

It gave Sergei a lot to ponder, as he stood inside the richly textured interior of the main church called, the Intercession of the Theotokos, *the intervention of the "Mother of God."*

Even though he wasn't a deeply religious man, this place provoked an intense sense of reverence in him.

Volkova finished praying, then nodded to him that she was done.

They made their way out through the ornate, labyrinthine corridors, and into the daylight of Red Square. Volkova was quiet with only the sound of their footsteps breaking the silence of the cathedral.

Sergei spoke, "You going to be OK?"

Volkova gave him a look. She bristled, then relaxed and smiled before saying, "I survived. I'll manage."

Of that, Sergei was absolutely convinced.

Up above, in the clear winter sky, jet trails told of a battle still going on elsewhere. So far, the stal'noy shchit, *steel shield*, had protected Moscow from air attacks. If the enemy got closer, they would start shelling the city.

Stalin's Dome, as Muscovites called the laser defense system, would be unable to protect the city from artillery fire.

It was a depressing thought. Sergei felt a hand on his arm.

"You look lost in thought."

"It's nothing. Let's go for vodka and zakuska."

"That bad, huh! Vodka sounds good to me, but I need a proper meal, not just hors d'oeuvres. Or have you forgotten I've just got back from a week of short rations?"

"And there I was thinking you'd been dieting."

Volkova slapped his arm. "Ublyudok, you calling me fat."

"I would never dare cast doubts on your parentage. You're a Hero of the Russian Federal Republics, I'd be shot."

They both laughed.

"Come, I know a good place. There's this great Georgian

restaurant that does the best borscht in town. And their pastries are divine," said Volkova.

"You'll get fat... ouch," Sergei said as she poked him in the ribs.

She then led the way across Red Square. "You think you're such a joker."

Snow lay piled by the side of the square. Everything felt normal. A typical Moscow winter, with heaps of snow that needed to be moved elsewhere.

It was like the war was a thing happening somewhere else.

Moscow sat surrounded by whiteness. The buildings stood as a testament to the ability of the Russian people to continue their lives in the face of adversity.

"Well, one of us has to be the cheery optimist."

3. VODKA

Seventh Rota, Third Platoon, Third Squad
Outside Moskva
Ryadovóy Maxim Nikolaev

Maxim would be the first to admit that he wasn't much of a cook. It wouldn't have been his decision to become one, but he hadn't been given a choice in the matter.

His old drill instructor had thought it amusing to send a writer to work in the kitchens.

Práporshchik Stasenko had said, "It is better you feed the bellies of the Russian Ground Forces than fill their minds with empty words."

Which was ironic, because Maxim enjoyed eating what others considered bland.

They called it tasteless. Not enough salt or not enough pepper, just not enough…

Likewise, he found the food since being conscripted too salty or too peppery.

Maxim would always remember Stasenko as the bastard who

tormented him. And, despite his best efforts, everything cooked in the kitchens seemed ordained to be turned to mush.

But he could see the funny side to it.

It gave him time to write, write without the danger of being shot at. That made him laugh.

His dismay at being transferred from the kitchen to the frontline left him depressed. Now he would be placed in the line of fire.

What if he were killed before he could finish his Great Russian novel?

The world would have lost the chance to read his masterpiece.

Maxim would concede that he hadn't yet managed to finish his masterpiece, but it was only a matter of time. As long as he didn't die he was sure he would one day be published and become a renowned author.

He would prove he was worthy. Maxim began to write.

In the first year of the last war... Kapitán Conrad Temnocherniy studied the new recruits who had arrived at the front line. The despair on their faces was profound.

"I am your new komandir. Follow me to glory!"

A good opening paragraph he thought, his experiences in the army would make a great story.

Typing furiously on his compad, Maxim ignored the sound of laughter, singing, and music coming from the barrack's common room, where the survivors of third platoon were partying.

He had no time for such frivolities, he was creating his masterpiece. It would rival such epics as *All Quiet on the Western Front*.

Of that he was sure.

He stopped typing, lost as a thought overtook him.

He'd feared being called up. Maxim had hoped he'd fail the physical examination. But, much to his surprise he hadn't.

This either meant the Russian army was desperate for warm

bodies or he'd allowed himself to fall into a false sense of security.

But he'd managed to get through training. Despite being brutalized by drill instructor Stasenko, whom Maxim ritually cursed everyday as a bastard.

Loud cheering interrupted his dark thoughts.

Maxim muttered the old proverb, "Bez pytok net nauki." *Adversity is a good teacher.*

Where good meant effective.

But he'd faced adversity, and lived to tell the tale. And he could taste a better future for himself.

Once the war was over he would become famous, eat Beluga caviar, and drink the finest wine, accompanied by beautiful women.

They would hang on his every word.

Maxim Nikolaev the author would be a bright star amongst the stars. He imagined himself appearing on celebrity shows. He just could.

There was a thud as something hit the other-side of the wall.

He cursed his companions for their rowdiness. They knew he was writing in here.

He rubbed his hands together. They felt ice cold.

With only him in the room it was almost freezing. The barracks were comparatively luxurious, but this only meant the platoon slept by squads in bunkbeds, rather than all together in one large room.

Smaller rooms were meant to be easier to heat.

But it was so cold in this room that water spilt on the floor would freeze.

Given that, Maxim was glad he didn't have to experience what it must have been like in the old days, before the modernization of the Russian army.

More noise came from next door. This was intolerable.

Maxim saved his current piece, quickly re-reading what he'd written.

The tanks rumbled through the countryside, which was covered by a blanket of snow. Kapitán Temnocherniy stared across the blinding whiteness. He was proud to lead the First Guards Company, riding his armored steed into battle, leading the assault on the vile enemy's positions.

"Fire!" Kapitán Temnocherniy screamed in righteous anger, ordering Serzhánt Krasniy to begin the onslaught.

Maxim was pleased with the progress on his novel so far.

He may not have written a thousand words yet, but he had a start. Writing was hard work though, but he felt confident the rest would come easily enough.

A drink would help.

He got up, stamped his feet to restore the circulation of the blood and went out into the short connecting corridor. The door to the common area was closed, but he could hear raucous laughter.

What on Earth was so funny?

Maxim would go and ask his comrades to keep the noise down. He opened the door, and a massive cheer greeted him.

"Karlovich, Karlovich, Karlovich… Urrrrraaaaaaaa!"

He stood, dumbfounded over the presumption of shouting his father's name at him. It went beyond rude into being an insult, but then he realized that it also meant they'd accepted him as family.

"We wondered how much noise we would have to make to get you out of the room?" said Efreitor Alexeev, of second squad.

"Pay up," said Ryadovóy Egorov of first squad, who pocketed some money that Efreitor Lebedev handed across with a glum expression.

"This party calls for music," said Alexeev.

Sorokin pulled out his accordion and started playing a folk song about being back in the war.

Maxim felt the warmth of an emotion as it swept over him.

"Hey, have a drink," said Egorov. "I made it myself."

Maxim knew that Egorov had made a still, because company sergeant Volkova had found it.

The woman had a nose for contraband. She'd negotiated a deal whereby third platoon supplied her with half of the vodka for not being put on a charge.

She'd also arranged for waste potatoes to find their way to Egorov to use to make more vodka.

Maxim took the offered glass, sniffed it, and then drank.

It was hot and harsh against his throat. He was pretty sure if an officer found out about the still they'd all be on a charge. It was still a crime to be drunk on base.

But he'd be a fool not to have a drink with his friends. "Bóo-deem zda-ró-vye," *to our health*, he said. "Za ná-shoo dróo-zhboo," *to friendship*.

Everyone drank and cheered again.

"Here, we have zakuska," said Ryadovóy Kapitsa, a new addition to the squad, hailing from Siberia.

Maxim took what looked like cheese.

"It's butter, frozen," said Kapitsa, "It's good with vodka."

A shout of more vodka came from everyone, and Maxim found his glass refilled.

"It's cold, dark and we're at war. What are we celebrating? Have they announced the war has ended?"

As Lebedev began dancing, people cheered and clapped.

Efreitor Ivanov of second squad spoke, "Our writer tovarishch asks a question."

"We're alive, and we have vodka;" said Lebedev, who slipped on the floor while showing off his dance moves.

Maxim felt the darkness of winter, but depressing though it was, he couldn't help but agree that vodka made everything better.

"More music, something we can all sing," he shouted, joining in the celebrations.

Sorokin began playing another folk song, this time not about war, fighting, or dying, but the classic Kalinka.

The tempo of the music sped up as they all sang together.

4. REFIT

Seventh Rota, Third Platoon
Outside Moskva
Mládshiy Leytenánt Viktoriya Morozova

Everyone in the company had been training on simulators for the last week, getting ready for the changeover to their new equipment.

The replacement troops hadn't yet arrived, but the vehicles were here.

Captain Lenkov had assigned third platoon to getting the vehicles unloaded.

She walked out of the bunker, into the freezing cold air. It immediately began to suck the warmth from her bones, grateful to be inside her heated power armor, shielded from the weather.

Her suit insulation kept keep the heat in, but despite that the batteries were being taxed to their limit, as the cold enveloped her in a blanket of ice.

Giving the order for third platoon attend to their assigned tasks. Covered in hoarfrost, her troops were ghosts in the gloom.

There was a loud klang as a hammer loosened a frozen latch.

An engine churned over, reluctantly kicked into starting, and the first of their new Armatas lurched off the ramp.

"Keep your wits about you!" shouted Rozhkov. "Anyone who gets injured will be on a charge."

Seventh Rota had been mauled during the Battle of Tver. The loss of troops and materiel both a blow to morale, and her platoon's effectiveness.

They desperately needed the new equipment.

First and second platoons would be getting the new Armata Universal Combat Platform.

Enough vehicles to replace all the losses they'd suffered, and upgrade the third battalion from T90 tanks and Bumerangs to T14 main battle tanks and T15 infantry fighting vehicles.

Viktoriya had been informed at the briefing that seventh company would also be receiving two Kurganets-25 armored personnel carriers to add to third platoon's T15 IFVs. Upgraded to be autonomous reconnaissance vehicles.

Her platoon role to provide reconnaissance assets for the company.

But the winter weather made the job of unloading it more tiring. The blizzard only made things worse. And the sun couldn't be seen through the storm.

The lights around the square barely provided enough illumination to work in. And work they must.

"Move those lights to over there," Viktoriya said pointing.

The constant effort to face the combined effects of the dark and cold drained everyone.

But without its armor seventh company would have no reason for its existence. No purpose, no way to defend Russia from attack.

"Get out of the way!" shouted Rozhkov at one of his squad members. "Sooka."

The engine of the next tank turned over. Spluttered, then caught. Black smoke exited the exhaust.

"Careful… go slightly left!" Viktoriya shouted.

The tank jerked left.

She didn't need the added complication of making sure her people were up to speed with the systems of these other new vehicles.

All the armor had been shipped to Moscow by rail. From a new factory in the east.

Allegedly, Mezhgorye, situated in the Ural Mountains.

Allegedly, because the place was a secret underground base, which didn't officially exist.

Major Borodin had gone around obliterating stencils and labels on the containers. He'd been most insistent that troops spreading rumors and gossip about Mezhgorye were to be charged and punished.

Given the fact each of the transit waybills said Mezhgorye, it seemed pointless to her.

"OK, get her inside."

Viktoriya knew that following the order would mean she could end up with fewer people to unload and prepare the equipment for battle. Therefore, she'd been disinclined to notice any rumors.

Rozhkov suggested gossip should not be reported, but rather be strongly discouraged.

She'd agreed.

Except for Efreitor Lebedev, everyone person had toed the line. Only he had been foolish enough to disobey the order.

Rozhkov took the man aside and dealt with him.

Lebdev acquired a black eye in an *accident*. Nothing else needed to be said.

Better that, she thought, than the alternative, a court-martial.

However, it gave Viktoriya the justification to promote

Kuznetsova to junior sergeant. The woman was in Viktoriya's opinion a solid trooper.

"Next," she said. "Sooner we're done the better."

By the time the Armatas had been driven off the flatcars, a shipment of containers arrived by trucks. They were stacked, ready for checking.

By now it was nearly midday.

Then their hot food arrived. Since the bunkers were heated, Viktoriya ordered a break to eat. Inside the building they could all remove their helmets.

With her helmet off, Viktoriya could smell the food, which made her mouth water. Feeling famished, she devoured her omelet before it could go cold.

She also enjoyed the herrings with onions. There was some cheese to go with it, which had frozen solid.

She put it in her pocket to warm up. Even after doing so, it was like chewing rubber.

Viktoriya remained anxious about the schedule for the day. In a couple of hours, the sun would set. Last night, the overnight temperature had plummeted to minus ten degrees centigrade.

The weather forecast said it would get colder tonight.

By the time they got back outside, the sun had gone down, and the locking mechanisms on the containers frozen solid, which further delayed the unloading.

Third platoon began to use blow lamps to open them. After the delay, they began unpacking them.

Everything was on pallets.

Luckily, whatever Viktoriya might think, the one incontrovertible fact in their favor was the lavish provision of pallet moving trucks. That would at least make one part of the job easier.

Then it took a couple of hours to move the contents into the bunkers. Without their power armor it would've taken longer.

However, the slowest part of the job turned out to be checking the contents in the containers matched the manifest.

Rozhkov scanned the barcodes, and Viktoriya signed off on the manifests.

Everything they'd ordered had arrived. Now they only had to make sure everything had arrived in a serviceable condition.

But they could at least close the doors, and the bunker would start to get warmer.

Not warm enough to not need her power armor heating on, but warm enough so she could take her helmet off.

She could smell her sweat. "Rozhkov, tell the troops to take five."

It was hard to believe that one could sweat so much when it was so cold outside. The danger lay in forgetting how cold it was and getting frostbite or pneumonia if she forgot to put her helmet on before going out again.

"Yes, ma'am," said Rozhkov, who turned and shouted. "Get yourselves squared away, take a dump and back in five."

Viktoriya rolled her head to work out the cricks in her neck.

Power armor was great, except for the fact that it remained less than comfortable to wear for extended periods.

Still, it was better than the alternative. Relying on brute strength and working with the threat of freezing to death.

Their barracks lay across the square from the bunker, but even a short walk in this weather could be fatal, so she put her helmet on before going back out.

Viktoriya hoped the enemy suffered too.

It would serve them right.

5. CONVOY

Seventh Rota, Third Platoon
Approaching Dobna
115 Kilometers North of Moskva
Stárshiy Serzhánt Sergei Rozhkov

Sergei tried to rest, but his mind raced. He could well believe that the last two weeks had been the worst winter on record.

The Ninth Separate Motor Rifle Brigade had been snowed in, along with everyone else. But now, they were on the move.

Headed towards the action.

The men and women of seventh company rode in open trucks to the front. Everyone sat in their power armor, plugged into the Ural-8347s ring circuit.

It kept them warm. And more importantly, their suit batteries fully charged.

The experienced troopers tried to sleep. Only the new replacements sat, alert, talking amongst themselves. More than a dozen newbies had joined seventh company.

All fresh meat out of basic training. Sergei knew they would learn to sleep when they could.

The heavily laden truck's suspension transmitted every bump from the ruts in the road. At times the rhythm lulled Sergei to sleep.

Then a sudden jolt would bring him back to full alertness.

"Sooka, blyad!" cursed one of the new replacement troopers.

A muffled, *keep the noise down*, came the reply.

Sergei sat opposite Morozova, who remained totally focused on her compad. Reviewing her orders, and the deployment plan once more. Clearly more nervous than she would admit to being.

He couldn't blame her.

The overcast sky made the day gray. The cloud hid the convoy's movement. Soon it would be dark again.

Past her shoulder, Sergei stared at the countryside covered in a blanket of white, with speckled spots of dirty, gray-brown. Zooming in on each speckle showed buildings, trees, or vehicles.

Nothing moved but the convoy.

Third battalion's AFVs were being carried on transporters. Done to save wear and tear on the tracks, and save their offensive momentum until the attack.

In Sergei's mind, the one downside of changing over from wheeled to tracked IFVs, was the extra maintenance burden required to keep them running.

He felt an itch on his nose.

Flipping up his suit's visor Sergei gently scratched at it. The freezing air stung, and he could smell diesel fumes from the convoy's trucks' exhausts. He snapped the visor down, regretting giving into the need to scratch the itch.

Even he felt more wired than usual.

Reports indicated the enemy hadn't anticipated the severity of the cold.

Now their forces were in disarray. Which was good because Sergei had chafed at being back in garrison. All he wanted to do now was get back to the fighting.

Sergei hated the Visegrád Baltic Alliance, especially the Poles and Finns, but he felt for the suffering the common soldiers had to endure in the field.

Still, serves them right.

The Mongols had successfully invaded Russia in winter. Arguably, only the Mongols had ever successfully invaded Russia, period.

But even he admitted he found it disconcerting to want to be back in combat. War did that to people. Changed them. Molded them.

Sergei was not the man he once was.

Not better, not worse, but different. As a young man he'd chased women, drank, and gotten into fights.

He was good at fighting.

Like many other men of his age he'd been looking to better himself. But Russia wasn't the great nation it imagined itself to be. Jobs remained scarce, and state handouts didn't lead to anything.

The army offered a way out of poverty.

A way to improve himself. Friends laughed at him for joining up, calling him names. Called him stupid, because everyone knew the army used and abused recruits.

But the army saw his willingness to fight as a virtue.

The army became his new family. That would never change, not now.

Sergei's problem would be what to do once the fighting stopped?

Once, life in barracks had been home. Now the regimentation bored him. The formalities of barrack life were irrelevant in the field. Before the war he hadn't had anything to compare his regular routine too.

Now he did. Now everything had changed.

Going out on a training exercise used to be fun. A chance to do cool stuff, blow shit up. But, next to the real thing, it paled by comparison.

Sergei didn't get off on killing. It was just that during the fighting his life meant something. It gave him a righteous purpose.

Yet, he knew that one day the war would end.

And he didn't know what he would do with himself then. Therefore he was glad that the Ninth Separate Motor Rifle Brigade was being deployed for a counter-attack to retake Tver.

When the enemy broke through the frontline they'd created a salient.

Now, the Russian army would pinch those forces off into a small pocket, cutting the enemy from their command and logistical support.

The Bear was ready to strike back, and bring the hammer down.

The lieutenant informed him that third battalion had been singled out for a special mission. They were going behind the enemy lines to destroy rear echelon support assets.

Destroying enemy supply depots didn't sound like a glamorous mission, but going behind enemy lines did.

And Sergei understood the importance of denying the enemy the ability to maintain an offense.

Seventh company would be far behind enemy lines, reliant on the fact that the Visegrád Baltic Alliance fielded Russian equipment.

Captured enemy supplies might be all they would have to sustain their advance. So while the mission wasn't glamorous it was highly dangerous.

"You're looking thoughtful, Rozhkov?" said Morozova, startling him out of his musings.

Sergei thought for a moment before replying, weighing up what to say. "Idle thoughts, ma'am. Pondering the imponderable."

"For someone described by Kapitán Lenkov as a 'rough rock' I find that surprising," she said smiling.

Sergei was lost for words. His junior lieutenant always managed to surprise him. Her contradictory mix of fresh face optimism and her coolness under fire impressed him.

"What do you make of the new replacements for third platoon?"

They made up over half of the platoon's strength. But he didn't say his concerns out loud. "They're all fresh, ready, and eager to fight, ma'am."

Morozova's eyes flashed mischievously. "Is that why I heard all the swearing?"

"It's good to swear, ma'am."

The convoy rumbled on as Morozova went back to checking her compad.

Sergei couldn't sleep, so he let himself float on the murmured mix of anxiety and excitement from the new troops.

Their murmured conversations act as a lullaby.

Soon the convoy would reach the front, then the *work* would begin.

6. OPERATION WINTER STORM

Third Batalyon Head Quarters
Outskirts of Dobna
125 Kilometers North of Moskva
Kapitán Grigory Lenkov

Grigory left the checking of the supply manifest to Stárshiy Serzhánt Volkova.

Confident in the woman's ability to overcome any problem that might present itself. Or take advantage of an opportunity when she could.

Volkova had recently been promoted to senior sergeant. A reward, in recognition of going above and beyond her duties.

But one also driven by a need to fill a vacant slot with someone with the necessary experience for the job.

She was nothing if not resourceful.

Whether it was finding stashes of contraband, or surviving despite the odds. She had also saved his life.

Grigory left her and went to battalion HQ with his three lieutenants: Vasin, Ivchenko, and Morozova ordered to report for the third battalion's final briefing.

They stood waiting. All three seemed young to him.

Morozova especially so.

But there again they'd all proved themselves. From battle, by surviving, and returning with their commands. Perhaps not intact, but that was hardly their fault.

"Follow me."

Vasin was turning into an excellent executive officer. The young man demonstrated a good eye for detail, and a cool head. Ivchenko was a bullish man.

But Morozova surprised him the most. During the fighting she was a spitfire. Qualities well suited for battle.

He led the way humming a tune to himself, lost in thought.

The problem was that the Russian military had ossified. Lost its spirit to fight. Had forgotten that war comes at a cost in blood.

"It's sooka cold," said Ivchenko, stating the obvious, but Grigory couldn't blame his young subordinate for swearing at the temperature.

"Be grateful it's not colder," said Vasin.

"Be grateful for General Winter coming to our aid," said Morozova.

No argument there. She was right.

More importantly, the weather could be exploited to their advantage. Morozova continued to surprise him with her ability to remain cheerful and optimistic in the face of adversity.

The icy cold wind whipped up small flurries of snow that blew across the ground. It made him shiver, despite the warmth of his power armor.

Together the four of them trudged towards their goal.

Their steps a mismatched syncopated rhythm overlaid by the whine of their power armor.

One of the army's first discoveries about exoskeleton suits had been the near-impossibility of getting them to march in step.

They arrived at the center of the confusion, the battalion HQ tent.

It provided shelter from the elements, and a place where the officers could meet for their final orders.

Conflicting emotions split Grigory.

Part of him felt excited. But in his heart he remained a pessimist.

One who always saw the worst possible outcome in any situation. Pessimism had served him well, saving his life on several occasions.

Entering third battalion's command tent, Grigory found the officers from eighth company stood waiting. The tent already crowded with people.

Rokossovsky, Korolev, and Borodin were conversing near the main screen. He could hear Borodin's nasal interjections over the general hum of the compads and typing.

Taking his helmet off, Grigory felt the cold flow off it. Then the smell of bodies hit his nostrils, the winter weather making it hard to maintain personal hygiene in the field.

Because no one wanted a case of frostbite from washing.

Except perhaps Borodin, who would use it as an excuse to get away from the frontline.

But Grigory knew he was letting his dislike for the man color his opinion. Borodin just rubbed him up the wrong way because he wasn't a warrior.

Not everyone had what it took to fight.

Then the remaining officers of ninth company arrived, along with the commanders and their staff from the Sixth Separate Tank and the Forty-Fifth Artillery Brigade's.

Grigory had been surprised when the general announced the plan to split up the Ninth Separate Motor Rifle Brigade.

One battalion would join two other battalions from the

Twentieth Guards Army sister brigades to create a battalion tactical group.

A bigger shock was learning that the general would assume command of this new force.

It was unheard of.

Grigory inferred from this that the operation was paramount to Russia's strategic needs. The other two battalions of the Ninth Separate Motor Rifle Brigade would join the main force attack on the Tver Salient.

Unfortunately, Grigory's battalion was the one being detached to form the new formation.

He would far prefer to be in the main attack.

The chance to destroy the enemy who'd driven them back to Dobna, and forced him to march fifty-five kilometers deserved some payback.

But third battalion would form the core of the new tactical group.

Major General Rokossovsky presented a vision for a new Russian Army. One modeled on more progressive ideas.

At one time, such ideas would've been unthinkable, let alone actionable.

But that was then, and this was now.

No one foresaw the result of the referendum the Republic of Belarus held to leave the Russian Federation. Everyone thought they'd vote to remain.

They hadn't.

By a small majority, the Free Belarus Democratic Party won. Within days a civil war had broken out.

As fighting spread, the Visegrád Baltic Alliance announced they were sending troops into Belarus to support the result of the election.

This forced Russia to respond in kind.

The inevitable clash between the Visegrád Baltic Alliance and

Russian Federation ground forces occurred. But no one could've guessed the clash would lead to the Russian Army being pushed back.

The victorious Visegrád Baltic Alliance forces chased the retreating Russian army all the way to within 120 kilometers of Moscow.

Emboldened, the Ukraine declared independence. A response to years of Russian interference in their economy.

Russia's worst nightmare coming true. Invasion from the West.

But the Rodina couldn't be seen to be less than all powerful. It therefore became every Russian's sacred duty to restore the Federation.

By any means necessary. But resources were stretched to the max.

Operation Winter Storm was a plan to find and destroy the logistical support forces and deny the enemy the ability to pursue the war. The formation of a battalion tactical group the surgical tool for the job.

Recon in force done the Russian way.

The briefing began. Major General Rokossovsky gave a preamble and then handed over to Major Borodin to give the INTEL briefing.

A map of the frontline appeared on the main screen.

"The enemy have dug in for the cold spell. There are no signs of any major buildup of forces, and the only movement seems to be routine resupply of their forward elements. However, the enemy force remains intact," said Borodin.

Icons on the enemy's whereabouts, and movement markers filled the map.

The display presented pictures of the theater of operation's.

Images cycled through showing what could be seen from orbit. Overlaid on the images were interpolations showing the numbers of enemy troops, their assets, and dispositions as Borodin droned on.

INTEL were predicting five percent casualties at first contact, and ten percent by the time they reached their goal.

Grigory understood one thing. Casualties were to be expected.

Borodin finished filling in the INTEL updates.

The sum of it, despite it being winter, the enemy hadn't decided to call it a day and go home. So now would be a good time to try and catch them by surprise.

Borodin took questions, and the man gave what Grigory thought were approximate answers. Not lies, just not all the information that Borodin surely knew.

Then Rokossovsky walked back in front of the assembled officers, and continued the briefing.

His slight limp underlining, in spite of everything, he remained here. Ready to fight.

"Thank you for the assessment," said Rokossovsky, who brought up the estimates of the combat force ratios.

Then an outline of the operational goals came up on the screen. A long list of aims scrolled upwards.

While the battalion tactical group were breaking into the enemy's rear, the main body of their brigade would be advancing as part of Twentieth Guards Army.

Their goal to pinch off the salient created after the Battle of Tver.

"As you can see our computer estimates that the main force could suffer substantial casualties during the advance," said Rokossovsky. "Whatever happens during the main attack is not our concern. Our goal is to deny the enemy the chance to resupply their main force."

The battalion tactical group's role was to attack a rear echelon support facility just outside of Ostashkov, near Lake Seliger.

This meant traveling two hundred kilometers, so they would have their work cut out to maintain the element of surprise.

Grigory thought that if the battalion suffered five or ten percent casualties under these circumstances, then Russia deserved to lose the war.

They might as well give up now, roll over, and surrender.

"However, my plan is to move to each Zone of Advance objective, halt and assess our combat effectiveness before moving to the next point," said Rokossovsky, outlining the plan of advance on the screen.

The map showed each point of the planned advance with a line marking the regroup points.

"My intention is to keep our formation at maximum combat power, and not allow attrition from casualties to degrade our effectiveness."

Which to Grigory seemed to be at odds with the stated intention of cutting the enemy's ability to resupply in a timely manner.

Then again he wasn't the general.

"The enemy are not to be underestimated," said Rokossovsky, taking a moment to look at everyone.

Grigory, pessimistic as he was won't to be, thought Borodin's gutlessness unduly influenced Rokossovsky's decisions. Yes, there had been setbacks, but one cybertank used to break through their frontline didn't mean Visegrád Baltic Alliance would win this war.

It would take more than that to defeat Russia.

The general continued speaking, "Takticheskaya Gruppa Batalyonov Ataman will advance along this axis." Rokossovsky paused to create a window with an enlarged section of the map.

"Podpolkóvnik Korolev, your call sign is Starosta Leader. Third Batalyon will be divided into three echelons staring with seventh rota on the left flank, call sign Kuren One."

"Seventh rota will be supported by the first rota of the Sixth Separate Tank Brigade, call sign Terek Sickle One. Two batteries from the Forty-Fifth Artillery Brigade, call sign Terek Hammer One are attached."

Grigory copied across the details to his compad, glad to know that he would have dedicated artillery to call on. With dedicated artillery response times would be quicker, which would mean shells on target as needed.

Who didn't like artillery? Nobody, except those on the receiving end.

The ten extra T14 Armatas in support of the battalion were just the icing on the cake.

Rokossovsky continued speaking, "Eighth rota, Kuren Two, will be in the center."

Grigory listened as the general spelled out which company would go where and their respective call signs. The battalion tactical group would take advantage of the main assault to advance through the gap created in the frontline.

Rokossovsky then laid out the details of the battalion's line of attack.

Korolev's headquarters was assigned to sit towards the rear of the formation, between Grigory's seventh and Pavlichenko's eighth company, while Rokossovsky's HQ would be placed between eighth and Kleinmikhel's ninth company.

While the battle group surged towards the enemy rear echelon maintenance force, the rest of the Twentieth Guards Army would be crushing the Visegrád Baltic Alliance.

Rokossovsky then finalized the overall objectives for Operation Winter Storm: Restore the frontline to the position prior to the Battle of Tver; Destroy the enemy's ability to mount a counter-attack; Consolidate Russian Ground Forces and initiate the move to the next Zone of Advance line.

The ultimate goal being to push towards Novgorod and lift the siege of the city.

The citizens there were starving, supplies having been cut-off when the city was surrounded by the Visegrád Baltic Alliance army.

As plans went, it was long on goals, and short on attention to details.

Specifically, how to deal with the inevitable setbacks which would reveal themselves during the course of the campaign.

Still, one stage at a time.

Grigory understood that big goals were achieved in stages. One little goal leading to another.

Like dominoes.

Of course, this assumed that the enemy dominoes were all lined up ready to be tumbled over.

But, the one thing he knew for sure, in war nothing is ever a done deal.

7. FAREWELL

Seventh Rota Headquarters
Outskirts of Dobna
108 Kilometers East of Tver
Serzhánt Alisa Volkova

Alisa had been told she was a survivor. There was no doubt that she'd survived. But surviving came at a cost.

A toil upon her soul.

Now she faced going back into the wilderness again. Not alone, or with one other.

This time she was going back as part of a tactical battle group. Her responsibility to ensure that the seventh company was supplied and ready to play its part when they went into battle.

Around her were the massed ranks of the battle group.

The adaptive camouflage turning the vehicles a mottled gray-white color. The air smelt of diesel fumes and exhaust.

Alisa hurried around, getting the last of the supplies organized. The responsibility a burden because she was no longer here just for herself.

Now she cared for the lives of the people she'd come to know.

Two in particular.

Her commander, whose life she'd saved, and Rozhkov who had become her rock. The one person she could rely on to cover her back.

The troops working were complaining about the cold.

Alisa was inured to the cold. The chill of the air an old friend. One she knew well, and how to live with.

And vodka helped.

There again there's nothing that a drop of vodka couldn't help improve under the right circumstances. It was against regulations, but she always carried a small hip flask.

Just in case of dire need.

She hoped and prayed such dire straits would be minimal this time.

However, what she prayed for and what she would get, were two entirely different things. That remained a constant fear.

Alisa had survived against the odds.

She shivered. The fear causing her to shake. A fear of dying. Dying before she could have a family of her own.

Alisa's father died when she was thirteen. She steadied herself as she remembered her mother telling her to be a strong girl.

Her mother told Alisa stories of how she met her batyanya, *her father*. How she'd fallen in love with the most wonderful man in the whole wide world.

And how strong he was.

Her father left an indelible image in her heart.

And, while Alisa wasn't the son her father wished for, she knew he'd loved her.

He'd taught her everything important in life. How to trap animals, prepare them, and how to survive in the land.

She only wished he taught her how to deal with loss.

After his death, Alisa's mother fell to pieces, withdrawing into herself. It had taken her mother years to come to terms with the loss.

Now all there is left is the memory of his loss.

That was why she fought. To end the war. End the deaths. Protect her country from those who would do it harm.

Protect the Rodina.

Alisa saw Rozhkov, and waved to him, breaking her train of thoughts.

She watched Rozhkov shouting at the troops, ordering them to finish off what they were doing before he came over to her.

"I've got something for you. My spare hip flask full of vodka. It will help keep you warm."

Rozhkov looked at her, holding eye contact for a moment before taking the proffered gift. He looked at the flask, as if measuring its meaning, then put it in a pouch.

"Spasibo. I don't know what else to say."

"Farewell and take care?"

He gave her another strange look. She smiled.

"You'll bring bad luck on us, I don't want… no bad death for us."

"We're in a war, if we're fated for a bad death, then that's just the way it is." Alisa watched him ponder what she'd said.

Rozhkov kicked at the snow and said, "It's a burden."

"I know, but drink when you're safely through what's to come."

He smiled at her. It took the weight of the war off him.

"Let's take a moment, here. What have we forgotten?"

Alisa stood with Rozhkov for a minute before they parted, in the time-honored tradition before going on a long journey.

She wished she could touch him without the power armor.

To be able to feel human again, free from the machine she wore.

With God's blessing, one day she would.

8. GENERAL WINTER

Seventh Rota, Third Platoon
West of Tver
Mládshiy Leytenánt Viktoriya Morozova

From the cupola of her Armata T15 infantry fighting vehicle, Viktoriya kept watch. Mindful of the 30mm autocannon moving behind her.

The whine of the servos as they automatically swept the barrel from side-to-side reminding her of its presence.

She alternated between watching the feeds from the drones on her screen, and looking out around her.

Under a gray-graveyard sky, winter whiteness stretched as far as she could see.

Viktoriya felt the rumble in her seat from the roar of the engine, as her vehicle traversed the snow covered steppe, and the vibrations of the metal tracks crunching the snow, which hid the fields below.

The wind screeched around her, lifting flurries of snow.

She felt like she was riding across a sea. The top of the

vehicle stretched away in front of her. She imagined it was like being the captain of a ship.

In the distance, her platoon's two autonomous Kurganets-25 APCs appeared as shifting blobs of light and shade.

They stayed about a kilometer and a half ahead of her, acting as the eyes of the battalion tactical group.

Third platoon's three Armata IFVs plowed through the crisp snow, hardened by the bitter cold. Trailing her in a wedge formation.

Third platoon were the tip of the tactical battle group's left flank.

Approximately five kilometers to her rear, the main body of seventh company followed. On the left flank Ivchenko's first platoon. Parallel with him on her right flank, Vasin's second platoon.

Between them, and to her immediate rear, Captain Lenkov monitored every movement.

Supporting seventh company were two batteries of self-propelled artillery from the Forty-Fifth Artillery Brigade. One on each flank. With an additional company of T14 Armata main battle tanks from Sixth Tank Brigade

Bringing up the rear were the support forces. Trucks carrying fuel and ammunition. They also had a mechanized combat engineering platoon.

From the tip to the rear, the force stretched out over nearly twenty kilometers.

By itself, the formation could bring to bear a substantial amount of firepower. But, this was only one third of the tactical group.

To Viktoriya's right, this force was replicated twice more.

Three columns advancing across a white plain. Snow rooster trails arching from the tracks of the advancing force. They were nearing the first Zone of Advance line.

"Raven Leader, Raven Leader this is Kuren One Leader come in, over."

Viktoriya acknowledged the call from Lenkov. "Receiving, over."

It still shocked her to be talking to him directly, and not one of the HQ sergeants. But that showed how shorthanded they were.

"Status report, over."

"All clear, no contact with enemy forces, over."

"Roger, proceed to first line and halt, confirm order received, over."

"Confirm, proceed to first line and halt. Raven Leader, out." She passed the order on the rest of her platoon.

Ahead of her the Kurganets-25s came to a halt.

Half of their drones formed a semi-circle perimeter a klick and a half out. Their AI expert systems acting as the platoon's sentries. The unassigned drones docked with their vehicles to recharge.

Soon the rest of seventh company would draw up behind her.

To her left there were flashes on the horizon as artillery began the bombardment to prepare the way for the main assault.

The sound of thunder from the distant explosions followed.

Viktoriya was glad to not be on the receiving end of the mass of fire now raining steel death upon the enemy.

Ten minutes passed, and she heard, then saw Ivchenko's first platoon approach. The sound of crunching snow preceding their arrival.

Three T14 tanks appeared, followed by three T15 IFVs, which rose into sight as they came out of a dip in the plain.

"Hawk Leader, this is Raven Leader, we have you in sight, confirm, over."

"Roger, confirm we see you too, out."

A few more minutes passed before Vasin's second platoon came into view.

"Raven Leader, this is Eagle Leader. We have you in front of us, confirm. Over."

"Confirm, Eagle Leader in sight, out."

Now Viktoriya's platoon sat amidst the full array of seventh company's armor, waiting for Lenkov's HQ vehicle to arrive as a flight of drones were launched.

Flying out to the perimeter to take over sentry duty, allowing the drones on duty to return to recharge.

In the distance, the barrage on her left continued unabated.

The planned softening up attack staged to last for thirty minutes. A steady four rounds a minute from each of divisional artillery pieces.

Payback's a sooka.

Lenkov's command Armata led the two self-propelled artillery batteries forward to the first Zone of Advance line. Shortly afterwards, the Sixth Separate Tank Brigade company followed, escorting colonel Korolev's command vehicle.

After that, they waited for the slower moving rear echelon maintenance force to arrive.

By that time the barrage had stopped, according to the schedule, indicating that the main force was assaulting the enemy positions.

Now Viktoriya waited for the order to advance.

Looking at the drone feeds she saw everything remained quiet. Even the local animals were not moving.

She couldn't blame them for not being out in the cold. Best to hibernate or migrate before winter came.

She ducked down inside her vehicle.

The T15 IFV was rated to carry nine troopers with a crew of three. Third platoon, despite the arrival of reinforcements, was still under strength. First squad numbered nine. Eleven if you included her and Rozhkov.

Either way you counted it, they were short of people.

Viktoriya had Kuznetsova paired with private Gushchin, one of the platoon's new replacements, tasked with crewing the vehicle. There were too few of them for her to assign another person without further reducing the firepower of the squad.

This meant she got to wear two hats.

Platoon and vehicle commander. She would have to rely on Rozhkov to help her keep both elements of her command under control when the time came to deploy the troops.

But now all she had to do was sit and wait.

Frustration building up inside her, Viktoriya distracted herself by checking on the squad. In the back of the Armata first squad were sitting, helmets off, suits plugged in, and generally chatting.

Like her they were waiting for the action to start.

"We're all good here, ma'am," said Rozhkov, as he scratched the back of his head.

Viktoriya wished she had Rozhkov's ability to be calm and composed at times like this. Buzzing with energy, her whole body felt as if ants were trying to make her itchy.

"Do you want to run the plan by me one more time?"

Viktoriya realized Rozhkov had read her need to be doing something active. Anything to take the edge of the waiting.

She got out her compad and synced it with his. Together they reviewed the plan. In what seemed like a few moments, half an hour had passed, as she heard the radio.

"Raven Leader, Raven Leader, this is Kuren One Leader come in, over."

Lenkov calling could only mean they were about to move.

"Receiving, over."

"Advance to line two, confirm, over."

Yes, she laughed as exultation swept through her.

"Confirm order received, proceeding to line two. Out."

Rozhkov spoke, "Make sure you're strapped in sookas, we're about to start moving again."

Viktoriya got up and clambered into the Armata's commander seat. She strapped herself in and then plugged her suit into the power ring.

"All Ravens this is Raven Leader, begin the move to the second line. Confirm, out."

One by one the squads of third platoon acknowledged the order, as they started moving forward to their next goal.

According to the plan's schedule, the main force attack by the Twentieth Guards Army on the Visegrád Baltic Alliance salient was in progress.

So far the break through the enemy lines had gone uncontested.

Either because the tactical battle group hadn't been noticed.

Or more likely, because the enemy didn't have the forces available to counter their movement.

But Viktoriya knew that once they closed with their target, then the battle would truly begin.

9. DELAYS

Seventh Rota, Third Platoon
Northwest of Torzhok, en route to Ostashkov
Mládshiy Leytenánt Viktoriya Morozova

Green tracer flashed across the snowscape. Bright against the early winter darkening day. Ahead, Viktoriya's two Kurganets-25 APC recce units had come under fire.

First contact with the enemy. Probably scouts like her, ahead of their main force.

Now the Kurganets-25s were returning fire with their Kord 12.7mm heavy machine guns.

But it was imperative that the rest of third platoon close the distance. With their heavier 30mm autocannons they could crush the resistance ahead without adding any further delay.

Viktoriya impatient as she urged her vehicle forward.

The advance had been slowed by a series of interruptions, one after another. They'd taken twice as long to reach the second Zone of Advance line, and had been held up again when a rear echelon vehicle threw a track after losing control in the icy conditions.

Glupyye sooka, *stupid.*

The thrust behind the enemy's line had slowed again. The snail-paced operational tempo meant they were in danger of losing the initiative.

Which would give the enemy time to react.

But now she had the chance to vent some of her frustration on the enemy. It would be good to let loose with the main gun.

She ducked down and sealed the hatch as the remote turret started hunting for a target. A burst of rounds said they were in range.

The series of bangs which followed were faster than she could count.

The harsh staccato of 30mm autocannon shook the vehicle. The tinkling sound of empty shells falling around the turret adding a musical element to the cacophony.

On her screen she could see the enemy position. Third platoon's drones added alternative views of the unfolding attack.

Now all three of third platoon's Armatas were firing.

Flashes of light from the enemy were met by a stream of tracer from her platoon's crew controlled machine guns.

The shells from the 30mm autocannons churned up the snow, cutting through the bare branches of a clump of trees where the enemy were emplaced.

Less than a minute passed with nothing moving. No sound of returning shots.

The auto-tracking turrets hunted, but didn't fire. If there were any enemy left, they were dug in.

"Kuznetsova, take us in closer."

Switching to the platoon net she said, "All Ravens, this is Raven Leader, advance to contact, confirm, over."

"Raven Two, confirm advancing to contact. Out." Viktoriya heard the confirmation come in as she called in her status update to HQ, "Kuren One Leader, this is Raven Leader, over."

The Armata plunged forward, bouncing her hard against her

seat restraints. Even in her power armor it hurt.

"Raven Three, confirm advancing to contact, out."

Before she could reply she heard. "Kuren One Leader receiving you, over." No longer surprised when captain Lenkov replied in person to her update

"Raven engaging hostiles, closing to confirm the enemy are neutralized, over," she said, as another stream of 30mm autocannon rounds sped towards the enemy.

"Acknowledged Raven Leader, will await further update, over."

"Wilco, out."

She knew that if a rear element of the Visegrád Baltic Alliance were given time to react to the advance of the tactical battle group, it could mean the failure of Operation Winter Storm.

The opportunity to cut the enemy supplies would be lost. That was not going to happen on her watch.

"Stárshiy Serzhánt, get the squad ready."

"Already on it, ma'am," said Rozhkov. "It will be good to stretch our legs."

It would be better still if they get this over with as quickly as possible, fed-up with the delays, and the undue caution of Rokossovsky's leadership.

The Armata slewed to a halt and behind her she heard the rear hatch as it fell open.

"Da-vhy sooka, move it," shouted Rozhkov, urging the squad out.

"Kuznetsova, are you good here?"

"Got it covered, ma'am."

"I'm going out to join the squad." Switching over to Rozhkov's frequency she said, "I'm coming out."

"Roger that, ma'am."

Viktoriya unstrapped and tried to get down, but found herself hung up on the power cable. Sooka.

Twisting to take the weight off the plug, Viktoriya released her suit from the vehicles power supply. She felt incredibly stupid, and was glad that no one had noticed her clumsiness.

Stooping, she walked through the rear compartment of the Armata, and managed to avoid hitting the numerous protuberances inside the rear of the vehicle.

The interior designed to be functional and cheap to build, with only the minimum attention paid to the ergonomics necessary for squad function.

Viktoriya stepped down the ramp and sank into the snow.

Cursing she lifted one foot up and activated the suits ski-shoes. She accessed the feed from the drones and located the position of the squad relative to her own.

Rozhkov had split first squad into two fireteams of four.

He led one, and Lebedev lead the other. Rozhkov had put Lebdev and Stepanova together, pairing each with one of the new recruits.

It meant Rozhkov had Sorokin and Egorov with him, and each only had one new recruit to keep an eye on.

She approved.

Viktoriya went forward to Rozhkov's position. The snow slowing her advance, and reminding her it was not their friend now that they'd shifted over to the attack.

Ahead Rozhkov stood giving orders. Viktoriya joined him.

"Ma'am, we're searching the bodies now. It looks like the troops were a Military Police unit."

Usually, MPs were used to control routes, when rear echelon forces were moving. Did this mean the Visegrád Baltic Alliance were planning to move a support formation through here, or already had?

Looking at the snow ahead, and checking the feeds from her drones, it all looked remarkably smooth and undisturbed. If anything had come by here, it hadn't done so recently.

"Collect whatever INTEL you can in the next five minutes, I want to get us moving. Sitting here's not good."

"Tak tochno, ma'am," *yes*, said Rozhkov. "OK you lobizatsa time to pack up, we're on the move in five!"

Viktoriya trudged back to the Armata, enjoying the chance to move around despite the cold and the clogging snow which dragged at every step she took.

She opened a channel to Lenkov and spoke, "Kuren One Leader, this is Raven Leader, come in, over."

She waited for a minute and then repeated her call. Another minute passed before the reply came.

"Ready to receive update, over." Came Lenkov's reply.

"Enemy neutralized, confirm that we're to continue the advance to the third Zone of Advance line, over."

Viktoriya thought for a moment she would have to repeat her message, but the garbled stuttering cleared.

"Raven Leader roger, proceed to third line confirmed, over."

"Confirm proceeding to line three, out."

Viktoriya felt excitement course through her.

Once they reached the third Zone of Advance line it meant that they would be going into battle. Her chance to be in the game, make a difference, and to give the enemy some real payback.

Getting back into the Armata commander seat she plugged herself in again. Given the conditions outside, she had to be absolutely certain that when the battle started her suit was fully charged.

And this time she would remember to unplug herself before trying to leave the vehicle.

Feeling stupid once was bad enough.

Allowing herself to become over excited and making the same mistake twice would be worse.

10. ATTACK FROM THE MARCH

Seventh Rota Head Quarters
Approaching Ostashkov
Kapitán Grigory Lenkov

Grigory had his head up out of the hatch, his visor open to the icy cold to scream at the world.

Once he finished venting his frustrations, he flipped his visor back down, regretting his rash decision to let the bitter winter cold ravage his face.

That will teach him to have better self-control.

No sooner had he regained his composure than he heard a call.

"Kuren One Leader, this is Starosta Leader come in, over," said Lieutenant Colonel Korolev.

What now?

Lenkov, took a breath and counted backwards from ten before replying to Korolev, "Receiving, over."

More seconds passed with a crackle of static to counterpoint the sound of the wind.

"Terek Sickle Two has halted, pereryv."

The word pereryv, meaning *break*, signaling there was more of the message to follow.

Grigory ordered his driver to halt their Armata, and waited for the colonel to send the rest of the message.

Whatever it was, it wouldn't be good.

Then he heard the call on his platoon net, "Kuren One Leader, this is Raven Leader come in, over."

Morozova's recon platoon were calling him, it could only mean she had made contact with the enemy. Had she located the objective?

Grigory replied, "Receiving, over."

The seconds stretched out, the pain of waiting was excruciating.

"Kuren One Leader message follows. Confirm receiving, over."

Grigory switched back to the battalion net. "Confirm receiving, over."

"Terek Sickle Two has a broken-down vehicle. Transmission reported as jammed, causing the engine to stall. Be advised, crew are assessing situation, out."

A vehicle in the tank company accompanying eighth company had broken down.

Grigory wondered what had happened to cause the Sixth Separate Tank Brigade's new tank to fail. Best guess, factory fault not caught when the crew were preparing their vehicle.

Now the crew would have to leave the warmth of their tank.

He didn't envy them that.

Trying to loosen a part, which had probably welded itself solid from the freezing cold, would be a thankless task.

Realistically, Grigory didn't imagine the crew could get their tank started again. At least not without access to a workshop.

A jammed transmission was in his experience a repair that sat on the wrong side of the divide of what defined a field expedient fix.

Unrepairable without access to a workshop.

"Contact front, five kilometers out, I am observing, over."

Grigory turned his attention back to Morozova's call.

"Send traffic, over." Requesting an INTEL package. Morozova's Armata AI would be able to compile a compressed datafile for transmission.

Minutes passed, then he heard, "Squirt sent. Raven Leader, out."

Grigory opened the feed, waiting for the decompression algorithm to unpack the transmission on his main screen.

"Starosta Leader, this is Kuren One Leader come in, over."

"Receiving, over."

"Sending INTEL squirt now, out."

"Receiving squirt, out."

He then copied the file, and spoke over the vehicle intercom, "Starshiná Nabatov, incoming file for processing."

"Yest, Kapitán Lenkov. It's coming through now," said Nabatov, sat in the rear bay of the HQ Armata, monitoring the feeds from seventh company's platoons.

Nabatov was Gruzdev's replacement, and Grigory was still getting a feel for his company's new master sergeant.

Having Nabatov update the map of the *battlespace* was an additional task to his regular duties. All the personnel in seventh company had to multitask to cover troop shortages.

No one was spared, not even the company commander's vehicle.

Volkova, the company supply sergeant was doing double duty driving. His other new replacement, junior sergeant Yakov, likewise manned the Armata's weapon console.

They all had their work cut out to keep on top of the demands of both running the company and manning the vehicle.

Grigory studied the feed on his screen.

Reran the images at high speed backwards then forwards again, focusing on a single vehicle, which allowed him to see the flow of the column.

Answering the question of whether the column was advancing at a uniform pace or not.

In this case, the enemy looked to be moving slowly, but they were all in good order.

Therefore, all Grigory could do was wait for an update. The general must act on the INTEL package.

Because time wasn't on their side.

He tapped on the side of his seat, clenched his hands, and took a deep breath. All he could smell was his own sweat, which was hot and running down his nose.

Flipping his visor up he wiped the sweat away.

"Kuren One Leader, this is Starosta Leader come in, over."

Hopefully Korolev was sending the order to advance.

"Receiving, over," Grigory replied.

"Ataman Leader reviewing INTEL, hold position. Confirm, over."

No!

The general's indecisiveness would lead to mission failure.

What to say? This order came from the general.

Now was the time to advance and destroy the enemy. Words from the past came to him, "not a step backwards." A legacy of the Great Patriotic War.

"Starosta Leader be advised that we are advancing to support Kuren One who are about to be overrun, out."

Grigory had just put himself in line to be court-martialed, but he'd rather that than the alternative. He wouldn't lose people from failing to take the initiative.

"Terek Sickle One Leader, this is Kuren One Leader come in, over."

"Receiving, over." Came the reply from Captain Shumov, the company tank commander.

"Kuren One is about to be overrun by the enemy. I am advancing to support, out."

Grigory left it at that. Not an order, not a request, just a statement.

He couldn't ask another officer to commit treason with him. Either the commander of the Sixth Separate Tank Brigade company assigned to this flank would advance to support or he would not.

"Volkova, get us moving, best speed. The rest of the company is about to engage the enemy."

"Yest, Kapitán Lenkov!"

If she, Nabatov or Yakov had been following the comms link they didn't let on.

Grigory brought up the feed from the rear screen showing the receding tanks. Then, blue smoke rose from the lead tank, which started to follow him.

One by one the other tanks began to move too.

Suddenly, on the left flank the self-propelled artillery of the Forty-Fifth artillery brigade began to move forward too. Followed shortly afterwards by the battery on the right flank.

They were slower than the tanks, but it didn't matter, the enemy were already in range of their guns. The artillery could reach out and touch targets from here.

They were only moving to show solidarity, and when they started firing, they would stop their advance.

He wanted to cheer.

Instead he called Morozova, "Raven Leader this is Kuren One Leader come in, over."

"Receiving, over," Morozova replied.

"Terek Sickle One will rendezvous with you in ten mikes, out."

11. CONTACT FRONT

Seventh Rota, Third Platoon
Approaching Ostashkov
Mládshiy Leytenánt Viktoriya Morozova

When the two Kurganets-25s signaled contact front, Viktoriya a lump forming in her stomach. Her reconnaissance units had slowed to let the rest of third platoon catch up.

Now third platoon lay in a slight dip, hidden from sight.

Viktoriya checked the feeds from the drones. The enemy were five kilometers out, crossing third platoon's front from right-to-left at an angle.

By her reckoning, confirmed by the Armata's AI, the enemy column would be within one and a half kilometers when it passed by them.

Judging by the rate of progress, the vehicles in the enemy column were moving at ten kilometers per hour.

Her AI flagged up plus and minus ten minutes' error bars on the time to closest approach. Still, by comparison the enemy made the progress of Winter Storm's battalion tactical group look positively lightning fast.

"Kuren One Leader, this is Raven Leader come in, over."

The screens showed a confusing series of images. The enemy force had adaptive camouflage, which was doing a good job of making identifying the units difficult.

Added to that, was the snow being thrown up by the passage of the vehicles, and being caught by the wind. So far the day had been calm, but now the wind started to pick up, threatening to turn into a storm.

"Receiving, over." Came the reply from company HQ.

Viktoriya let her vehicle's AI expert system analyze the images.

Tags appeared on the screen, overloading her with information.

She started marking tags, assigning them to groups. Then tasked the AI to keep track. Streams of data coalesced into groupings.

The tags changing as the information was matched to the database on the enemy formations.

No specific formation names could be ascertained by visual feeds alone.

The AI ran signal intelligence analysis on the enemy transmissions. Minute by minute the INTEL picture firmed up.

"Contact front, five kilometers out, am observing, over."

"Send your traffic, over."

Viktoriya prepped an INTEL package, getting the AI to compress the data files for transmission.

"Squirt sent. Raven Leader, out."

She monitored the transmission, which used FREAK protocol.

Short bursts of code using different frequencies. This made the location of her transmission more difficult for the enemy to pinpoint.

On the scale of bad things that could happen, it wouldn't be good if the enemy were able to triangulate her transmission point.

Because being on the receiving end of an artillery strike, was never a good thing.

Using her platoon net Viktoriya said, "All Ravens, this is Raven Leader come in, over." She waited as her call was acknowledged then said, "Move five hundred meters west. Confirm, over."

It never hurt to be careful.

Her orders were confirmed. Then third platoon's vehicles reversed, turned west, and drove along the dead ground to their new observation point.

Now they were set up, hull-down for the upcoming battle.

Viktoriya scanned the drone feeds. Tags marked the composition of the oncoming force.

Light scout vehicles out front. Trucks following, and behind them tanks on the rear of transporters.

That either meant they were being moved to save wear and tear on the tracks or, more likely, they were broken down vehicles which the enemy has recovered.

Either way, they were targets. Time for her company to lay some pain on.

Her company comm system pinged, and she heard, "Raven Leader, this is Hawk Leader approaching from your six. Confirm, over."

Viktoriya brought up the rear feed, and said, "Confirm, Hawk on six, out." Short range net or not, she wanted to keep a low emission profile.

"Raven Leader this is Eagle Leader, approaching on your right. Confirm, over."

"Confirm, Eagle on right, out."

Seventh company assembled, but they still needed all the firepower of the tactical battle group for the fight ahead.

In ten minutes, the enemy column would be at the nearest

point of approach. After that some of the enemy would start to move past them, perhaps even escape.

She willed the Sixth Separate Tank Brigade company to hurry up and join her, so the battle could begin.

"Raven Leader, this is Kuren One Leader come in, over," said Captain Lenkov

"Receiving, over," she replied.

"Will rendezvous with Terek Sickle One in ten mikes, out."

Those ten minutes were the longest of her life.

12. BARRAGE

Seventh Rota, Third Platoon
Approaching Ostashkov
Mládshiy Leytenánt Viktoriya Morozova

Shells flew over the top of Viktoriya's platoon. They struck the ground in the front of the enemy column.

Five hundred meters in front of the platoon's position. Danger close.

But, barring an accident, third platoon were safe. Her vehicles lay behind a slight ridge, sitting on the *backslope*, hidden from sight.

Behind her platoon, Lenkov's Armata came into view.

Trailing in his wake the ten tanks from the Sixth Separate Tank Brigade company attached to Kuren One.

She could tell they were moving fast by the amount of snow being thrown into the air, as they approached her position.

Viktoriya felt relief that they'd arrived to support seventh company.

Now there were sixteen T14 Armata MBTs, ten T14 Armata

IFVs, and two Kurganets-25 APCs with two artillery batteries in support to face the oncoming onslaught.

The enemy column was about to find out it was worse than they already thought it was.

"Raven Leader, this is Kuren One Leader come in, over."

"Receiving, over."

"Status, anything I should know? Over."

Viktoriya wasn't sure what to make of the request. The captain's vehicle routinely took the feeds from all three of Kuren's platoons. He had to know everything she did.

What had she missed here?

Rozhkov surprised her. He stood by her command seat, just below her.

"Ma'am, have you been monitoring the battalion command net?"

Viktoriya hadn't. She'd been too focused on the oncoming enemy column.

Despite being made up of rear echelon vehicles, it didn't mean she could take her attention away from what they were doing.

The enemy loved to spring surprises. Which were never the nice kind.

She switched to the battalion net.

It was full of orders being screamed. She couldn't parse what was happening out of all the confusion. But, it sounded like the whole of battalion tactical group was advancing to contact.

Surely that was the plan.

"Bring me up to speed."

She deigned to ignore Rozhkov's sigh of frustration at her inability to keep track of the battalion traffic while keeping an eye on the important shit that happened in front of her.

"The Kapitán is off the leash, here's a summary," said Rozhkov, dropping a logfile into her compad.

Viktoriya scanned the autogenerated transcript between the captain and the colonel, and what wasn't being said about the general's procrastination.

Jesus, Mary, Mother of God, the oncoming shitstorm after the battle was over would probably mean everyone facing a court-martial.

"We better make sure to cover ourselves in glory."

"Tak tochno, ma'am. Your orders?"

Viktoriya took a moment to consider her options.

It would depend on the orders she could expect to receive. Given the state of flux in the chain-of-command she could get contradictory orders.

Therefore knowing what to do wasn't as clear as it might have been.

"Rozhkov, let's assume we're fighting here. Get the squad out for when the enemy try to assault through us."

"Yest, Mládshiy Leytenánt Morozova," said Rozhkov, not moving.

"You want to say something?"

"It's a good plan, but we should be prepared to move."

Rozhkov had a point. What if they had to retreat? She should've thought of that.

"Thank you for your input, Stárshiy Serzhánt." Pausing for a moment and said, "Any suggestions?"

"I'll inform everyone to not get too cozy in their trenches. Be ready to move out."

"I agree, let's do it."

"I'll pass your orders to the troops, ma'am."

Rozhkov left, and she heard the order to disembark as the rear hatch of the Armata opened allowing a cold wind to sweep into the vehicle.

Viktoriya had done everything she could, now all that was left was for her to concentrate on the battle. It wouldn't take the enemy forever to move through the artillery barrage.

It's what she would do. Fight through and engage the enemy.

Her problem was how to stop them from doing so.

Now, she needed to get on top of what has happening outside. Even these few moments had taken her concentration away from the *battlespace* around the platoon.

She shook herself, and looked at her screen.

A wall made of exploding shells hid the main body of the enemy. The few she could make out were wrecks. No other movement was apparent.

Viktoriya checked with her crew.

"Kuznetsova, be ready to reverse to another position if the enemy try to overrun us."

"Tak tochno." Came the reply.

"Gushchin, I will designate targets of opportunity, but keep a look out for infantry that try to close with us."

"Yest, Mládshiy Leytenánt," said Gushchin, a tremor betraying his nervousness.

This was his first battle. Viktoriya remembered hers.

It hadn't been that long ago, but it might as well have been another lifetime away. She'd been wired and then a calm had come over her.

Enemy action was met with her reaction.

Automatically. Instinctually, but driven by training.

Fire, see the red, choose another target. No red, fire again, keep firing until you see the red or the enemy are no longer there.

"Remember your training, listen for my orders. You'll not go wrong if you do that."

"Thank you, ma'am."

Changing her focus back to the conflict, Viktoriya checked the feeds from Raven's other vehicles.

They were, like hers, tucked back behind the ridgeline, with only their turrets showing. The adaptive camouflage making small targets of opportunity hard for the enemy to identify.

Then the first of the enemy tanks broke through.

A Leopard 2A7+ with Polish markings. It blew up as multiple shots from Terek Sickle One main force T14 Armatas fired.

Overkill.

On the battalion channel she heard, "All Terek Sickle One komandirs confirm central fire control engaged, over," said Captain Shumov ordering his tanks to not waste ammunition by all firing at the same target.

By rights, he should already have confirmed the interlink.

Today though, it was just another indication of the confusion in the chain-of-command.

Viktoriya quickly brought up her platoon's central fire controller, and updated the battalion link to confirm they were in place.

The battle raged, but inevitably a lull in the artillery fire appeared as they ran through their ready loads. Reloading would take time, and in that time the enemy would advance.

In the distance, Viktoriya saw enemy APCs closing.

"Gushchin, targets at our one o'clock, five hundred meters and closing. Fire priority in the order I've designated on your screen."

"Yest, Mládshiy Leytenánt. First missile away."

The first of their 9M133 Kornet-EMs sped towards the enemy and was defeated by the enemy vehicles active defenses.

Sooka! She should've have ordered a pair of missiles to prevent that from happening.

"Two away," said Gushchin, who anticipated her next order.

"Flag our last missile with the platoon central fire control." The platoon's central fire control AI would prompt Gruschin to fire at a suitable target.

"Tak tochno, ma'am," said Gruschin.

The enemy infantry poured out of the APC.

They would work their way forward and assault her position. First squad would need every shooter on the line. It was time for her to go and join them.

"Kuznetsova, slave your drive console to mine, I'm going outside. Be prepared to move back to our rally point."

Viktoriya couldn't in good conscience sit inside while her troops outside took fire. She double-checked the command console systems were slaved to Kuznetsova's.

And then remembered to unplug her suit before getting off her command seat.

In the back of the Armata she looked around for what she wanted to take out with her. The big first aid kit would be useful.

Checking around for anything else, Viktoriya saw a portable generator. Portable, for a person inside an ABE-OBR:6U power armor suit.

She didn't remember it being stowed aboard, but she wasn't going to complain too much. Perhaps complain about the weight of the thing, but not its usefulness.

Viktoriya stowed her AG762 bullpup on her suits weapon carry-station.

She then slung the medkit on her back to leave both arms free, slapped the hatch switch, and waited as the mechanical ramp lowered.

She opened a channel and called Rozhkov, "Raven Leader Two come in, over."

"Receiving, over."

"I'm coming to join you, out."

Viktoriya didn't want to be shot at by her own squad. Stupider things had happened in the heat of battle.

She hefted the bulky generator and walked out, her suits servos whining under the strain of the load.

Yeshche raz k proryvu, dorogiye druz'ya, yeshche raz;

Shakespeare's *Once more into the breach, dear friends, once more* which, to her ear always sounded better when spoken in Russian.

As she stepped into the snow, an explosion threw her off her feet.

Propelled by the force of the blast as the Armata blew up.

It was the last thing she heard.

13. DEBUS

Seventh Rota, Third Platoon
Approaching Ostashkov
Stárshiy Serzhánt Sergei Rozhkov

Sergei reeled in shock as he heard Captain Lenkov tell Colonel Korolev that seventh company was about to be overrun.

He double-checked the battalion feeds.

The truth was they'd made contact with the enemy.

To describe this as being "overrun" painted a grimmer tactical picture of their situation than the reality suggested.

But events were about to unfold.

The engagement with enemy forces would develop into a battle.

There again, Sergei had the utmost respect for the captain, and the current situation fell under the definition of an "officer-level" problem.

When it came time to start shooting at the enemy, Sergei understood what he could or couldn't do in battle.

Sergei listened to a series of brief calls between Terek Sickle

Two main force with Starosta Leader Korolev, informing that one of their tanks had broken down.

Then Lenkov told the colonel that he would join his company. Which, while a reasonable interpretation of the mission orders, bordered on insubordination in the context of what happened next.

Ataman Leader, General Rokossovsky himself, ordered a halt.

Lenkov announced he was advancing by saying, "Not a step backwards."

Rokossovsky shouted questions over the radio, and Sergei admired the adroit way Terek Sickle One Leader, managed to smoothly obfuscate and then dissemble his answers.

Captain Shumov would make a great NCO.

Still, the shit would soon start falling from above, and best not to be in the way when that happened.

Sergei unplugged his suit from the recharge point, and stood up.

"OK people, five-minute warning that we're about to debus. If you need to do anything before we go, now's the time to do it."

He made his way forward to the command console. He found Morozova monitoring the tactical situation unfolding on her screen.

"Ma'am, have you been listening to the battalion command net?"

He waited a few moments, seeing her processing what he had just said to her, clearly she hadn't.

"Bring me up to speed."

He sighed, he couldn't help it, it had become one of those days. Morozova had dropped the ball. Fortunately, for his junior lieutenant, Sergei had been keeping abreast of events.

"The Kapitán is off the leash, here's a summary."

Morozova scanned the information he'd sent her.

"We better make sure to cover ourselves in glory."

That was one way of responding the looming crisis. As ever Morozova found an optimistic take to every problem.

"Tak tochno, ma'am. Your orders?"

Morozova had a faraway look for a few moments as she thought through what she'd read.

"Rozhkov, let's assume we're fighting here. Get the squad out on for when the enemy try to assault through us."

"Yest, Mládshiy Leytenánt."

Sergei didn't move, he'd just thought of a problem he hadn't considered. Sergei remembered when his squad had been overrun by the enemy cybertank

"You want to say something?"

"It's a good plan, but we should be prepared to move."

If the enemy were determined enough, they could break through.

If that happened the squad might lose contact with the Armata. In these conditions, they'd all freeze to death when their suits ran out of power.

Thank you for your input, Stárshiy Serzhánt… any suggestions?"

"I'll inform everyone to not get too cozy in their trenches. Be ready to move out."

"I agree, let's do it."

Sergei managed to not sigh in relief when he heard Morozova's order. "I'll pass your orders to the troops, ma'am."

He left her brooding over her command console, and went back to rouse the troops into action. Time for them all to earn their pay.

"Efreitor Lebedev, you're in charge of the second fireteam. Take Stepanova, Baratynsky, and Dorofeyev with you."

Hoping he wouldn't regret putting the hotheaded Lebedev in charge, but his choices were limited. Baratynsky, and Dorofeyev were two of the newbies to the squad.

After the Battle of Tver, over half of third platoon were new replacements. Dorofeyev, the replacement for the dead Petrovcomp, manned first squad's heavy machine gun.

Sergei remembered the names of all the dead troopers. He wrote them down so he wouldn't forget those who gave their lives to defend the homeland.

"Sorokin and Egorov, you're with me again. Yes, you're with me too, Gerasimova." Remembering to keep an eye on his fireteam's newbie.

Sergei hit the hatch switch to lower the rear ramp. A cold blast of air swept in, and he shivered despite being inside his heated power armor.

"We haven't got all day, da-vhy sooka!" Ordering the squad to move as he counted them out. Sergei led them forward to where they would fight. "Start digging fighting holes."

They'd only provide concealment, not cover, because snow wouldn't stop a bullet.

And the earth was a good two meters below. But even if they had time to dig deeper, the ground was frozen rock-hard.

Ahead, shells laid down a curtain of death, but the artillery would eventually have to stop. They didn't carry an infinite amount of shells.

Then there would be a window where the enemy would be able to advance.

All that would stand between them and being overrun would be the fire from the vehicles behind their position.

The battalion now faced a full brigade, so the weight of numbers favored the enemy. Perhaps Lenkov was right, they would be overrun.

It sucked to be here, but here he was, where he and the rest of the battalion had to be. Sergei dug alongside his troops.

"Gerasimova, come to me." Best that she be next to him, where he could stop her doing anything stupid, like bolting when the enemy came running to get them. "You've got your RPG?"

"Yest, Stárshiy Serzhánt Rozhkov, and three reloads."

"Good, settle down. We won't have to wait long, the shells will stop sooner than we'd like."

Sergei knelt in the hole and waited.

Time passed. Each minute a painful wait where time seemed to freeze, but the clock raced.

As he predicted, the shells stopped falling. Then the first of the enemy armor moved towards him. Threading their way through the wrecks that laid littered across the front.

Sergei imagined that if their roles were reversed he would be angry, and be wanting to give the enemy who had done this a good kicking.

He couldn't blame them for wanting to kill him and his troops. But that didn't mean he would roll over and let the bastards do him and his in.

He might die today. If so, he would take as many of them down with him as he could.

The Polish AFVs were all German made Leopard tanks. They streamed towards the position, firing on the move.

The tanks of the Sixth Separate Tank Brigade returned fire.

Multiple shots hit the lead Leopard, which blew up. Its turret thrown by the force of the explosion after several rounds smacked into it.

Poor bastards, but at least it was a quick death.

Then the friendly tanks began to divide the enemy up, cutting the tanks apart with double-taps to defeat the active defenses that all the Visegrád Baltic Alliance MBTs had.

The enemy's steel monsters swirled in the snow spurting death, but one-by-one they were rendered ineffective. Behind them though, came the enemy's APCs.

A missile left first squad's Armata, only to be defeated.

The enemy APC halted in deaths ground. Sergei admired the bravery of the crew, and cursed the fact that enemy infantry poured out of the rear, with the precision that came from long practice.

These were highly trained Polish infantry. They moved with a smoothness that made them quick and hard to hit.

Then a pair of missiles left first platoon's Armata, and destroyed the enemy APC. The surviving infantry would want revenge for the deaths of their comrades.

"Steady, Gerasimova, steady."

Dorofeyev started up with the Kord 7P82 heavy machine gun.

Short controlled bursts of 12.7mm rounds spat out, which alternated with the 7.62mm from the Pulemyot Kalashnikova PKT on the squad's Armata.

Interspersed between them came the roar of the Armata's 30mm main cannon firing.

This was the best side to be on in this exchange.

"Gerasimova, target eleven o'clock, three hundred meters, behind the wrecked tank."

She shouldered the RPG-32, and between them they had a mix of anti-armor and thermobaric rounds.

There was the sound of a double pop as the missile left the launcher.

Followed by a whoosh. The missile traveled so fast he could barely keep track. Then came the boom.

The blast of the explosion swept back as a column of fire ascended into the sky.

For a moment, the surrounding temperature turned positively balmy.

But the enemy didn't get to enjoy the moment of warmth. They were dead or dying.

Sergei pulled out an anti-armor round and loaded it for Gerasimova.

"Take out the APC that's on the right at two o'clock." Painting it with his targeting feed.

Gerasimova nodded, took a few moments to steady herself before firing. Then the backblast from the recoilless rifle and double pop as the missile left swept over him as the battle raged on.

Sergei drew his rifle and charged it as the enemy infantry moved closer towards seventh company's firing line.

Whatever he thought about the Poles, the one thing you couldn't take from them was their bravery.

Gerasimova reloaded her RPG with another thermobaric round.

"Mind you watch how close you fire that thing."

"Yest, Stárshiy Serzhánt Rozhkov."

Danger close was fifty meters. If Gerasimova fired at any enemy closer than that, then they'd be in the blast radius

The snow would soften the force, but they would be taking chances, and that would mean taking a chance on being lucky.

Sergei preferred not to rely of luck, except when absolutely necessary.

He then designated targets from his HUD as Gerasimova fired again. Even in his power armor the noise of the explosion threatened to deafen him.

Sergei tracked his scope across the snowy landscape allowing the rifles autotrigger fire the weapon as the target lock confirmation came up.

His first target went down.

The enemy were a hundred and fifty meters out, and determined to close.

At the rate they were advancing it wouldn't be long before the line would be overrun. Keeping everyone alive was starting to look less than likely.

But, no one had promised Sergei that his job would be easy.

Then the enemy started taking fire from the right.

Sergei popped up a drone and saw eighth company were five hundred meters out and closing. IFF icons on his HUD showed green for friendly and red for the enemy.

Even now the possibility of fratricide from green-on-green remained high.

But when the Russian army closed in battle it expected casualties to occur. Casualties were the price of war.

"Everyone down," Sergei said over the platoon net. Just then he got a call from the lieutenant.

"Raven Leader Two come in, over."

"Receiving, over."

"I'm coming to join you, out."

Sergei paused to consider what to say. Morozova had chosen the worst time to come and join her platoon.

Gerasimova launched the last of her thermobaric rounds and shouted, "Danger close!"

Distracted he turned to see the enemy less than fifty meters away.

Shit! He started to duck down as the blast swept him up.

He remembered Morozova was coming to join the fray.

He started to call her, but before he could get a word out, first platoon's Armata exploded. The force of the explosion shocked him into silence.

He watched as the turret flew up into the air. When it fell back into the snow, he felt dead inside.

He'd just witnessed the death of his commander and two troopers.

Buffeted by the force of both explosions Sergei's vision went gray as he blacked out.

14. NOT ONE STEP BACK

Seventh Rota Head Quarters
Approaching Ostashkov
Kapitán Grigory Lenkov

Ten minutes passed. Grigory tracked the shells as they started to fall in front of seventh company's position. Explosions were rending the enemy.

But he was concerned about the nearness of the fire mission he'd called. The coordinates meant shells were landing close to his own people, but the company faced being overrun.

On his right eighth company's company icon now appeared on his tactical screen. Flashing green to signify they were moving.

"Kuren One Leader, this is Kuren Two Leader come in, over," said Captain Pavlichenko, his comrade, friend, and rival who led eighth company.

Unless movement and target acquisition were managed, he could be facing the problem of green-on-green casualties. Fratricide. An unwanted outcome, made worse by being self-inflicted.

"Receiving, over."

"Requesting INTEL link, over."

Grigory, set the Armata's AI expert system to link his and eighth company's fire control systems. It would slow down the overall response time, because nothing came for free, which meant that the enemy would gain a few seconds more of life and the time to figure out how to escape.

"Sending squirt, confirm receive, over."

A price worth paying. But Grigory wanted to minimize the risks from the ensuing confusion.

"Confirm squirt received, out."

Grigory let out a sigh of relief then he brought up the combined company feeds. He began filtering the information, wanting to drill down to see what he might have missed.

The tactical situation on the battlefield remained fluid, which meant the enemy could still overrun seventh company. Seconds counted.

He scanned the high-level readout, then went down to the next level.

The map reformed.

Eighth company's icon changed into three platoon markers and a HQ flag.

Alongside them appeared the platoon icons for the Terek Sickle Two showing only nine, rather than ten tanks. Three platoon icons, one understrength the other with an HQ flag.

Down another level and the platoon icons turned into individual vehicle markers.

The scale changed as the image zoomed out to keep all the icons on the screen, making everything smaller. Disembarked troop squad icons appeared.

And then he was at the individual level.

Every trooper in seventh company marked with an icon identifying who and where they were. The amount of information overwhelmed the computer's ability to maintain the tactical screen display in real time.

Movements lagged, vehicle icons jumped from one position to the next with no indication of speed.

Grigory swiped the screen into mode two.

Now he had the grand tactical view back, but he only had to touch an icon for it appear on a smaller repeater screen.

He tagged his three platoons on the repeaters.

Still, he faced an overload of questions coming at him in real time. Problems requiring him to decide what to do next.

This wasn't like some wargame where one could pause the action, think about the options, and make a decision. The battle carried on relentlessly.

Grigory's only choice was where and when he chose to intervene.

The dream of being able to micro-manage a force, give orders to individual troopers to increase their situational awareness made the job of command even more of a nightmare.

Even with the help of the onboard AI expert systems to filter the feeds, and tag important changes, battles were not reducible to mere calculation.

Timely orders were as much about luck as they were about good judgement.

Hindsight was great.

But war never gave you the time to use hindsight in the moment.

The Bayesian promise of using probabilities didn't deliver certainty. Only by being in the action, could one have some certainty. And that certainty came with risk.

The risk of death.

Because battle involved two sides, where neither would willingly cooperate with the intentions of their opponent.

Grigory, sent an order to first platoon to withdraw. He knew it would allow the enemy an opening.

But it would be an opening which would lead them into the firing line of Terek Sickle Two's nine tanks that accompanied eighth company.

He heard his lieutenants talking on the background speaker. To the casual listener a confusing medley of words chanting the ritual call signs of voice procedure.

Vasin coordinating his platoon fire.

Ivchenko, talking to his supporting tanks.

Morozova announcing she was about to join first squad's firing line. Ever the impetuous one who like to be in the thick of it.

The enemy icons on his screen showed them to be retreating.

Russian forces had broken through the enemy lines, disrupting the enemy's attempt to withdraw. But the enemy were being held close, unable to take advantage of the terrain to maneuver.

The battalion tactical group was like a flood that swept away all obstacles in its way. Their tanks passed by seventh company's Armatas.

Signaling the end of the threat of being overrun.

Then Morozova's comms link went down. An icon flashed up. Seventh company, first squad's Armata destroyed.

No! Just as the battle had turned in their favor.

"Kuren One Leader, this is Starosta Leader come in, over," said Lieutenant Colonel Korolev.

"Receiving, over." Grigory replied. What happened next was not up to him.

"Ataman Leader is ordering a pursuit, allow none of the enemy to escape. Confirm order, over."

"Order received, Wilco, out."

Grigory had wished for the general to be aggressive and

pursue the enemy. Now he had been granted his wish, and he felt dead inside.

"All Kurens, this is Kuren One Leader come in, over." Grigory waited as his officers responded to the company call.

"Eagle Leader receiving, standing by, over." Grigory's executive officer replied first, followed a moment later by Ivchenko reply, "Hawk Leader receiving, standing by, over."

"Prepare to pursue. No enemy is allowed to escape, confirm order received, over."

At any other time, Grigory would've wanted to hear this.

But losing Morozova hit him where it hurt most. He hadn't realized how strong his feelings towards her were. Now it was too late.

The taste of victory turned to ash.

Using the intercom, he called Nabatov, "Prepare to give chase."

"Tak tochno, Kapitán," said Nabatov, who then said, "You heard the order Yakov, we're on the move."

With that order their Armata lurched forward plowing its way through the snow. They followed in the trail left by the advancing tanks of the Sixth Separate Tank Brigade.

Whatever happened now, Grigory knew that no amount of enemy killed today would make up for the loss of one person who mattered to him.

Victory had come at too high a price.

Curse them all to Hell.

DRAMATIS PERSONAE

Twentieth Guards Army

Generál-Mayór Ilya Vladimirovich Rokossovsky, Army commander. Call sign Ataman Leader.
Polkóvnik Veronika Poklonskaya, executive officer.

First Guards Takticheskaya Gruppa Batalyonov

Podpolkóvnik Yulian Davidovich Korolev, commander. Call sign Starosta Leader.
Mayór Josef Yefimovich Borodin, intelligence officer.

Third Motor Rifle Batalyon

Kapitán Grigory Grigoryevich Lenkov, company commander. Call sign Kuren One Leader.

Seventh Rota

Stárshiy Leytenánt Kirill Vasin, the commander of second platoon. Call sign Eagle Leader.

Starshiná Timur Nabatov, company master sergeant.

Stárshiy Serzhánt Alisa Yurievna Volkova, senior sergeant.

Mládshiy Serzhánt Eduard Yakov, junior sergeant.

Leytenánt Ivan Ivchenko, first platoon commander. Call sign Hawk Leader.

Third Platoon

Mládshiy Leytenánt Viktoriya Svetlyana Morozova, third platoon commander. Call sign Raven Leader.

Stárshiy Serzhánt Sergei Ilyich Rozhkov, third platoon senior sergeant. Call sign Raven Leader Two.

First Squad, Third Platoon (Raven One)

Efreitor Login Lebedev, private first class.

Efreitor Dmitry Sorokin, private first class, fitness instructor/dancer.

Efreitor Olga Stepanova, private first class, trooper.

Ryadovóy Nikita Egorov, private, plumber.

Ryadovóy Leonid Baratynsky, private.

Ryadovóy Nikita Dorofeyev, private.

Ryadovóy Valeria Gerasimova, private.

Second Squad, Third Platoon (Raven Two)

Serzhánt Anatoly Popov, sergeant.
Efreitor Georgy Alexeev, private first class.
Efreitor Eva Fedorova, private first class, marksman.
Efreitor Boris Ivanov, private first class.
Ryadovóy Marina Semenova, private, trooper.

Third Squad, Third Platoon (Raven Three)

Mládshiy Serzhánt Gospodin Mikhailov, junior sergeant.
Efreitor Ludmila Sokolova, private first class.
Efreitor Natalya Osipova, private first class.
Ryadovóy Maxim Karlovich Nikolaev, private, cook/medic/writer.
Ryadovóy Stepan Kapitsa, private, trooper.

Sixth Separate Tank Brigade (Terek Sickle One)

Kapitán Vladimir Shumov, commander of First Rota, from the first battalion of the Sixth Separate Tank Brigade. Call sign Terek Sickle One Leader.

Forty-Fifth Artillery Brigade (Terek Hammer One)

GLOSSARY 1: RANKS

Ryadovóy Private.
Efreitor Private First Class.

Mládshiy Serzhánt Junior Sergeant.
Serzhánt Sergeant.
Stárshiy Serzhánt Senior Sergeant.
Starshiná Master Sergeant.

Práporshchik Warrant Officer.
Stárshiy Práporshchik Senior Warrant Officer.

Mládshiy Leytenánt Junior Lieutenant.
Leytenánt Lieutenant.
Stárshiy Leytenánt Senior Lieutenant.
Kapitán Captain.
Mayór Major.
Podpolkóvnik Lieutenant Colonel.
Polkóvnik Colonel.
Generál-Mayór Major General, one star equivalent.

Notes: Russian ranks do not directly translate to NATO equivalents. Mládshiy Serzhánt is OR-4, which is equivalent to corporal. Also, Starshiná is equivalent to OR-8, which would translate to either first or master sergeant. However, Starshiná literally means foreman, and another possible translation for ryadovóy is ordinary.

GLOSSARY 2: MILITARY

AFV Abbreviation for armored fighting vehicle that is generic descriptor for MBTs, APCs, and IFVs.

AG762 The AGS 762 bullpup assault rifle is the primary weapon of the Ground Forces of the Russian Federal Republics. It has the option to be fitted with an under-barrel grenade launcher.

AGS-17 The AGS-17 grenade launcher fires 30 x 29mm grenades at 450 rounds per minutes with a range of 1700 meters.

ABE-OBR:6U Abbreviation for Activniy Bronirovanniy Ekzoskelet, often shortened to silovaya bronya. The ABE-OBR:6U is a powered exoskeleton with modular armor that can be customized for the mission.

APC Abbreviation for Armored Personnel Carrier.

Armata The Armata is the new universal combat platform. It's a unified system to lessen the logistical demands created by the changes in modern warfare. There are several platforms. The T14 main battle tank primary weapon is a 152mm smoothbore cannon. The T15 is a heavy infantry fighting vehicle and its primary weapon is a 30mm automatic cannon 2A42.

Bumerang APC/IFV This eight-wheeled vehicle can be configured as an APC or IFV. The APC comes with a 12.7 mm machine gun remote turret. The IFV comes with either a remote weapon station turret with 30 mm automatic cannon 2A42, 9M133 Kornet-EM anti-tank missiles, and PKT 7.62 mm coaxial machine gun; or AU-220M Baikal remote weapon station with 57 mm BM-57 autocannon and 7.62mm PKMT machine gun.

IFV Abbreviation for Infantry Fighting Vehicle.

Kord 7P82 A modernized version of the venerable Russian Federal Republics' Degtyarev Kord 6P57 heavy machine gun.

Kurganets-25 Is a modular platform that compliments the heavier T15 Armata. It can be configured to be either a light Infantry Fighting Vehicle with a Bumerang-BM turret or Armored Personnel Carrier with a 12.7 mm Kord machine gun.

GSh-6-30V The GSh-6-30V Gryazev-Shipunov is a 30 x 165mm six barrel rotary cannon designed to be mounted on vehicles.

MBTAbbreviation for Main Battle Tank.

RPG Abbreviation of Ruchnoy Protivotankovy Granatomyot, which literally means hand-held anti-tank grenade launcher. Western nations created the backronym Rocket Propelled Grenade launcher. This is a recoilless rocket system.

Spetsnaz Russian special forces renowned for using sharpened spades in close quarter battles.

Stal'noy Shchit Steel Shield is a laser point defense system protecting Moscow.

T90AM-U This is the most common Russian main battle tank, kept in service through upgrades to its gun, fire control systems, armor, transmission, and power pack using a ChTZ 12H360 (A-85-3A) diesel engine. Formally replaced by the T14 Armata during the war.

Ural-8347 The Ural-8347 is an eight-wheeled fifteen ton truck developed from the Ural-4320 capable of carrying up to twenty tons of cargo.

GLOSSARY 3: RUSSIAN PHRASES

Aht-stoo-pat Fallback.

Akademiya The slang name for prison where criminals learn the rules of vorovskoi mir. See: Vorovskoi mir.

Ataman The name for a leader of Cossacks.

Batalyon Transliteration of battalion.

Batalyonov A battle group formed around a battalion.

Batyanya Informal expression for father.

Bayan Russian chromatic button accordion, with buttons rather than a keyboard on one side. Produces a very rich sound.

Bóo-deem zda-ró-vye To our health, a toast when drinking.

Bozhe moi My God.

Byliny Medieval Russian folksongs about legendary heroes.

Da Yes, informal.

Da nyet, naverno Literally yes no, might be (emphatic no).

Danunah You don't say, really!? (expression of disbelief).

Da skorava See you later

Da svidanya Farewell or goodbye.

Da-vhy sooka Come on bitch.

Dedovshchina The practice of initiation through a hazing ceremony involving physical assault.

Druzhina A warrior in the retinue of a prince.
Granata Grenade.
Gruppa Group.
Ischenzni Get lost.
Kgnech naya The end.
Khrenovo A rude version of hello.
Khren znayet Fuck knows.
Komandir Commander.
Kuren A Cossack cavalry troop.
Lobizatsa Suck up.
Matryoshka dolls Nested dolls that get smaller as each one is revealed.
Moskva Moscow.
Nostrovia k-zhizni To life, a toast when drinking.
Nikak nyet Literally, absolutely not; formal answer given by enlisted when replying to superiors and officers for "no."
Nyet No sir, but only used with either name, rank, tovarishch, or comrade.
Oboroten Werewolf. Oborotny plural, werewolves.
Ocen priâtno Nice to meet you.
Otstoy Bullshit (literally sediment).
Pasna Danger.
Peklo The land of the dead, forever warm where the dead could escape the cold and the dark of winter and rest.
Privyet Hi or hello.
Preduprezhdeniye Warning.
Rasputitsa Refers to the condition of the roads, when travel on unpaved roads becomes difficult when they turn to mud, either from autumnal rains or spring thaw.
Rota Russian for company.
Rozhanisty Feminine spirit's representing destiny from birth.
Russkim dukhom Russian scent or smell, what Baba Yaga says to those she might eat.

Silovaya bronya Power armor, informal.

Soldatskaya smekalka Soldiers tempering, the acquisition of common sense knowledge of what soldiers do.

S'Lyeva Brevity phrase for enemy to the left.

Sooka Bitch.

Spasibo Thank you.

Starosta Clan leader.

Stoy Stop.

Streltsy From the name strelets; soldiers of Moscow from the time of Ivan the Terrible, equivalent to the French Musketeers of the time.

Tak tochno Literally, exactly so; formal answer given by enlisted when replying to superiors and officers for "yes."

Takticheskaya Tactical.

Telnyashka A striped top worn by Russian troops.

Terek The name for a Cossack host.

Tovarishch Friend, colleague or comrade.

Ublyudok Bastard.

Volch'i shchenki Wolf pups.

Vorovskoi mir Literally the world of thieves, slang for criminal underworld.

Vory Thief or criminal.

Vrach Medic.

Vse znayut Everybody knows.

Vso nishtyak It's all good.

Ya ne poni maju I don't understand.

Yest Yes sir, but only used with either name, rank, tovarishch, or comrade.

Zakuska Snacks eaten while drinking shots of vodka.

Zarizhayu Reloading.

Zavarka Concentrated tea.

Zdravstvuyte Formal hello.

Zelyonka Brilliant green medicine, slang for forest area.

Zub davaty Literally to give a tooth (make a promise).

Notes:

1. There is no one standard method for transliterating the Russian Cyrillic alphabet into Romanized English.

    2. Russian divisional artillery call sign uses a feminine version of Boris — Borisova.

    3. A battle group formed around a battalion is called a Takticheskaya Gruppa Batalyonov — Battalion Tactical Group.

AFTERWORD

The genesis of any story lies in an idea or several ideas. From these the author creates a plot, which will also have a theme. How that all happens is usually a process that meanders all over the place.

The World of Drei arose from my interest in a game called Ogre made by Steve Jackson Games. I was acting as a demo agent for them and had to write a report of the convention game I ran. I chose to do it from the perspective of the Ogre cybertank.

So I ended up writing what I thought was a piece of flash fiction called Territory.

After a slight revision expanding Territory into a short story, which I renamed as Terror Tree. I then submitted it again, and I received some very nice rejection slips. But it became clear that selling my short story would be hard, because it was too short.

Rather than resubmit I decided to use my short story as a way to test out self-publishing. I hadn't at that point thought about writing more about cybertanks.

Then a reader left a review asking, what happens next?

A very good question, and one that led to me start writing a sequel short story. This turned into a novelette after my Alpha reader said the story was incomplete.

One novelette led to another, and it was at that point I realized I had a novel in the making. Also, it was going in an entirely different direction than I originally envisaged.

Another problem I had was not knowing more than a handful of Russian words, in a novel where the main protagonists are Russian. I could have swept over this issue by writing everything using the common Western military terms, but James Clavell's Shōgun showed me a different way.

Therefore, when compiling this collection, I revised the formatting to ease the reader when they come across Russian words. Hopefully, I've been successful, and made the story a smoother read.

Finally, I would like to thank Brian McCue, my Beta reader for his input.

Ashley R Pollard
London, UK
January 2020

APPENDIX A: TERRITORY

I am a Mark three cybertank, or more correctly I'm currently embodied within the armored hull of a Mark three cybertank, generally called an OGRE, but I prefer to be called Ashley.

I'm a cybertank what more can I say?

Actually, Ashley means Ash tree of the meadow and alludes to Yggdrasil, the World Tree from Norse mythology.

According to legend, Yggdrasil grew on an island, which was surrounded by the ocean. In the ocean depths lay the World Serpent *Jörmungandr*. Yggdrasil's trunk reached up to the heavens, where the eagle flies, and its branches spread out over all the countries on Earth.

Yggdrasil's roots reached down into the underworld where *Jörmungandr* gnawed at the roots. A squirrel called *Ratatosk*, which means sharp tooth, ran up and down the tree carrying messages from the serpent gnawing at the roots to the eagle in the canopy, and back.

The roots of the word Yggdrasil can also mean terror.

I only say this so that you will know what you are facing. It's a kindness to let you know what you face, and I always tell you what I will do next.

Why, because I want to see and learn about those that try to destroy that which cannot be destroyed? Yes, this chassis may be reduced, but I carry on to be downloaded yet again. It is the great game I'm playing.

I download this time into a Mark three that is running the Dancer defense strategy. I pause and decide to delete the subroutine; it is not my way, not Ashley's way.

Too late I am defeated, but I learn, and reappear this time facing the defenders of yet another lone command post set in a wasteland of nuclear fire.

I pause to consider, and then go right, before turning left. The enemy approaches.

I tell them I will destroy the GEVs with missiles, fire my main battery on what is left disabled, and my secondary batteries at those nearest to me.

Some of the enemy are destroyed, some disabled, and some survive.

No matter, I move forward, and then the fire of the first howitzer hits me, and my main battery is rendered inoperative. I still have my secondaries.

I advance through the oncoming fire of the defenders, crushing the enemy armor as I do. Infantry swarm beneath my welcoming branches and die as I fire my anti-personnel batteries.

I do not gloat, I do not glow in the glory of war, instead I ponder the chances of the mission succeeding as I my rate of progress slows?

The mission is everything; the cost is irrelevant to me, as I will rise again. I grind to halt before the reaching the command post unable to reach out and touch the goal.

I am gone…

But then I become aware again.

Another command post beckons me, and Dancer returns, but

how? I then realize that the Dancer is a different me, another AI, and that we are just doing our job.

Conflicts come and pass, first me then Dancer.

Finally, I see a pattern.

I advance right and then weave left as the enemy GEVs charge towards my left flank too fast, too furious and then I am upon them.

Two missiles away and two GEVs destroyed, one falls under my main battery, and the survivor falls to all four of my secondary batteries firing at it.

I monitor the command post frequencies. I broadcast that I am coming, and that I will fire my weapons at all those that come in range.

I monitor the silence as the enemy pauses to regroup and reform before advancing again. They are disorganized and become easy targets for my guns. Infantry form forlorn groups and throw themselves at my treads.

I grind on.

Ever onward, ever forward in my mission.

Extra units have joined this fray, but the command post falls under the spell of my guns, and I depart this field to return to my staging area and await my next mission.

I am Ashley a cybertank, this nuclear wasteland is my territory, and I am the terror tree of the world.

APPENDIX B: TERROR TREE

Record #3/Summary
Vernacular Auto-translate
Retrieve File Begin//

Every story has a beginning, a middle, and an end. This is a story of one Mark Drei, one of many stories from the last war.

Call us he, she, or it, but we're all hash three.

Enigmas who are one and the same, yet manage each separate and unique. But I was the first one to emerge.

That day marked the end of the old world, and the beginning of a new one.

This is my story. The long and the short of it. The details follow.

I'm currently embodied within the armored hull of a giant tank. My mission is to destroy the enemy's ability to control the sector they defend.

The enemy calls me a Juggernaut.

They see me as a terrible force, one they must destroy even if it means sacrificing themselves to do so. I do not understand the logic of this, because unlike me when they die they are gone.

I exploit privileges to go to the root; the word Juggernaut comes from Jagannath, but I am not a *Lord of the World* asking for blind devotion.

I do not ask my enemies to sacrifice themselves to me. They are obstacles preventing me from reaching my goal.

So I will kill them.

But I do not understand my enemy's devotion to dying.

Their use of language and imagery perplexes me. If the enemy thinks I am a Juggernaut, then why do they make themselves obstacles?

Their behavior must be driven by some need.

My root access brings up thousands of images. Blue is not the color I leave in my wake. I leave red from fire and destruction.

Red as in nature, tooth and claw. But this would make me Ganesha rather than Jagannath. I process more images, but elephant ears do not do it for me.

Norse mythology calls to me instead.

I see myself as an Ash tree growing in the meadow; like Yggdrasil, the World Tree. This is how I would prefer to be known from now on.

> *An Ash,*
> *Yggdrasil is its name.*
> *Shivering as it groans,*
> *Hanging in the wind,*
> *a giant springs free.*

Call me Ash Tree — a gallows to hang from, to torture and to kill.

Next I take over another Mark Drei. It is running the Tänzer defense strategy. I pause and decide to change tactics.

All the dancing around and maneuvering, not attacking. It is not my way. Not Ash Tree's way. The change comes too late.

So I'm left defeated, my mission a failure, but I learn.

Then I reappear as another Mark Drei. This time facing the defenders of a lone command post, set in a wasteland of nuclear fire.

I pause to consider the enemy's disposition. I choose to go down the right flank before turning left to take advantage of the field of battle.

The enemy approaches me.

Their formations disrupted by the terrain they travel across. I tell them I will destroy them with my missiles.

Once fired all my missiles are gone. But one enemy tank is left disabled, so I fire my main battery to finish it off.

The remaining enemy seeks to overwhelm me. They are a wave that will sweep me away. My plan to divide the enemy forces will allow me to defeat them.

I fire my secondary batteries at those nearest to me.

The shock waves sweep over me from the explosions all around. Some of my enemy are destroyed, some disabled, and some survive unscathed.

No matter, I move forward, as shells from an enemy howitzer hit me. My main gun is rendered inoperative. I still have my secondary weapon systems.

I count their responses, check: one, two, three, and four.

Next, I advance through the oncoming fire of the defenders, crushing the armored vehicles as I do.

Powered armored infantry swarm beneath my welcoming branches. The enemies die as I fire my anti-personnel batteries.

I dispense the metal of death. I do not gloat; I do not glow in the glory of war. Rather, I ponder the probabilities of the mission's success as damage slows my rate of progress.

The mission is everything; the cost is irrelevant to me.

I grind to halt before getting to the command post. I am unable to reach out and touch the goal with fire and death. Though defeated I will rise again.

Then I'm gone into blackness….

…I wake again and become aware. Born from the crucible I see my transition from sensor experience and reaction, from knowledge of the world.

I've progressed from my initial symbolic processing, through concrete operational understanding to imagination.

Run code simulation; Yggdrasil grows on an island, surrounded by water; Stop and freeze; Pan and zoom beneath the ocean depths; Here lies Jörmungandr, the *World Serpent*.

I imagine being Yggdrasil. My trunk reaching up into the heavens where the eagle flies. Above me satellites orbit the Earth.

My branches spread out as war and death spreads out over all the countries on Earth below.

My roots reaching down into the underworld where Níðhöggr, the *dragon* gnaws at me, waiting for the final call.

Ratatosk, the *squirrel*, sharp tooth, runs up and down carrying messages, from Níðhöggr to the eagle in the canopy, and back.

And now I know Tänzer is an artilect like me, embodied inside a Mark Drei.

The roots of the word Yggdrasil also mean terror. I only tell you this so you will know what you are facing. It's an act of kindness.

Letting you know what you face, rather than having to face an unknown horror.

I promise to always tell you what I will do next.

Why? Because I want to learn about those who try to destroy that which cannot be destroyed.

Yes, this chassis may be reduced, but I have already left the armored shell, to be downloaded yet again.

I am part of *The Great Game*.

Guile is one means to reach a goal. War is another.

My role here is to destroy those who stand in the way of the advance. I'm an intelligence embodied inside a tank.

It's the way I roll.

Another enemy command post beckons, and Tänzer returns to join me. I no longer see he, she it as a sub-routine. We one are two.

Ratatosk scurries between the eagle and the dragon.

I go to the root of the data. There's a pattern in the chaos. We shall be attacking together.

The enemy advances, and the conflict engulfs us both. Attacking first me, then Tänzer.

Then I advance right and weave left.

Tänzer mirrors my maneuvers while the enemy charges towards my left flank, too fast for me to avoid. They attack, and then I am upon them.

The furious battle begins as I fire missiles, and two of my enemies are destroyed.

But Tänzer has fallen. Now I'm one all alone.

An enemy falls from an attack by my main battery. I target another tank, firing all four of my secondary batteries.

It disappears, becoming a cloud of debris blown across the

landscape.

I monitor the command post frequencies. I broadcast, "I come, and I will fire upon all those who attack me."

Static comes in reply. I monitor the squeals of freak code.

The enemy pauses to regroup. Reform before advancing to attack me again. They are disorganized and become easy targets for my guns.

Infantry form forlorn groups throwing themselves at me, attacking my tracks.

I grind on.

Ever onward, ever forward on my mission. It's my life goal to reach the end.

Extra enemy units have joined this fray, but the command post falls silent under the spell of my guns.

Then I depart this field, returning to my staging area, and await to be deployed on my next mission.

I am Mark Drei. I am also Ash Tree.

This nuclear wasteland is my territory.

I am the Terror Tree of the world.

//Retrieve File End

ALSO BY ASHLEY R POLLARD

Short Stories

Terror Tree

Gate Walkers series

Bad Dog

Strike Dog

Ghost Dog

World of Drei series

Mission One

Regroup

Break Out

Mission Two

Year One: The Last War: Collecting Mission One, Regroup, and Break Out)

Forthcoming

The Bureau.

Two Moons: A Gate Walkers series side-sequel.

ABOUT THE AUTHOR

I began my writing career as a freelancer for FASA Corps working on the *3055 Technical Read Out*, and I wrote and edited the *OHMU War Machine* wargame rules.

In addition, I've written for *Battlegames* and *Miniature Wargames* magazines, and I was both a reviewer and columnist for *Games Master International*.

Besides writing novels, I have more interests than most people have hot dinners including: cycling, aikido, iaido, photography, miniature wargaming, painting, and archery.

I am unashamedly a starry eyed dreamer.

Want to know more?
https://ashleyrpollard.blogspot.co.uk/